HOME IS THE HANGMAN,
HOME FROM THE STARS

"The Hangman explored Io for us, and started in on Europa. Then it started behaving erratically, just when we thought it had really learned its job."

"That sounds right," I said.

"It refused a direct order to explore Callisto, then headed out toward Uranus."

"Yes. It's been years since I read the reports . . ."

"The Hangman's ship crashed or landed, as the case may be, in the Gulf of Mexico," he continued, "two days ago."

I just stared at him.

"It was empty," he said, "when they finally got out and down to it."

"I don't understand."

"Yesterday morning," he went on, "restaurateur Manny Burns was found beaten to death in the office of his establishment, the *Maison Saint-Michel*, in New Orleans."

"I still fail to see . . ."

"Manny Burns was one of the four original operators who programmed—pardon me, 'taught'—the Hangman."

The silence lengthened, dragged its belly on the deck.

ROGER ZELAZNY

HOME IS THE HANGMAN

A TOM DOHERTY ASSOCIATES BOOK
NEW YORK

HOME IS THE HANGMAN

Copyright © 1975 by Roger Zelazny

Home is the Hangman had its first book publication as part of *My Name is Legion* by Roger Zelazny, published by Ballantine Books, a division of Random House, Inc., in 1976. Used by permission of the author and Ballantine Books.

A Tor Book
Published by Tom Doherty Associates, Inc.
49 West 24th Street
New York, N.Y. 10010

Cover art by Martin Andrews

ISBN: 0-812-50983-8

First Tor edition: May 1990

Printed in the United States of America

0 9 8 7 6 5 4 3 2 1

Big fat flakes down the night, silent night, windless night. And I never count them as storms unless there is wind. Not a sigh or a whimper, though. Just a cold, steady whiteness, drifting down outside the window, and a silence confirmed by gunfire, driven deeper now that it had ceased. In the main room of the lodge the only sounds were the occasional hiss and sputter of the logs turning to ashes on the grate.

I sat in a chair turned sidewise from the table to face the door. A tool kit rested on the floor to my left. The helmet stood on the table, a lopsided basket of metal, quartz, porcelain, and glass. If I heard the click of a microswitch followed by a humming sound from within it, then a faint light would come on beneath the meshing near to its forward edge and begin to blink rapidly. If these things occurred, there was a very strong possibility that I was going to die.

I had removed a black ball from my pocket when Larry and Bert had gone outside, armed, respectively, with a flame thrower and what looked like an elephant gun. Bert had also taken two grenades with him.

I unrolled the black ball, opening it out into a seamless glove, a dollop of something resembling moist putty stuck to its palm. Then I drew the glove on over my left hand and sat with it upraised, elbow resting on the arm of the chair. A small laser flash pistol in which I had very little faith lay beside my right hand on the tabletop, next to the helmet.

If I were to slap a metal surface with my left hand, the substance would adhere there, coming free of the glove. Two seconds later it would explode, and the force of the explosion would be directed in against the surface. Newton would claim his own by way of right-angled redistributions of the reaction, hopefully tearing lateral hell out of the contact surface. A smother-charge, it was called, and its possession came under concealed-weapons and possession-of-burglary-tools statutes in most places. The molecularly gimmicked goo, I decided, was great stuff. It was just the delivery system that left more to be desired.

Beside the helmet, next to the gun, in front of my hand, stood a small walkie-talkie. This was for purposes of warning Bert and Larry if I should hear the click of a microswitch followed by a humming sound, should see a light come on and begin to blink rapidly. Then they would know that Tom and Clay, with whom we had lost contact when the shooting began, had failed to destroy the enemy and doubtless lay lifeless at their stations now, a little over a kilometer to the south. Then they would know that they, too, were probably about to die.

I called out to them when I heard the click. I picked up the helmet and rose to my feet as its light began to blink.

But it was already too late.

The fourth place listed on the Christmas card I had sent Don Walsh the previous year was Peabody's Book Shop and Beer Stube in Baltimore, Maryland. Accordingly, on the last night in October I sat in its rearmost room, at the final table before the alcove with the door leading to the alley. Across that dim chamber, a woman dressed in black played the ancient upright piano, up-tempoing everything she touched. Off to my right, a fire wheezed and spewed fumes on a narrow hearth beneath a crowded mantelpiece overseen by an ancient and antlered profile. I sipped a beer and listened to the sounds.

I half hoped that this would be one of the occasions when Don failed to show up. I had sufficient funds to hold me through spring and I did not really feel like working. I had summered farther north, was anchored now in the

Chesapeake, and was anxious to continue Caribbeanward. A growing chill and some nasty winds told me I had tarried overlong in these latitudes. Still, the understanding was that I remain in the chosen bar until midnight. Two hours to go.

I ate a sandwich and ordered another beer. About halfway into it, I spotted Don approaching the entranceway, topcoat over his arm, head turning. I manufactured a matching quantity of surprise when he appeared beside my table with a, "Ron! Is that really you?"

I rose and clasped his hand.

"Alan! Small world, or something like that. Sit down! Sit down!"

He settled onto the chair across from me, draped his coat over the one to his left.

"What are you doing in this town?" he asked.

"Just a visit," I answered. "Said hello to a few friends." I patted the scars, the stains on the venerable surface before me. "And this is my last stop. I'll be leaving in a few hours."

He chuckled.

"Why is it that you knock on wood?"

I grinned.

"I was expressing affection for one of Henry Mencken's favorite speakeasies."

"This place dates back that far?"

I nodded.

"It figures," he said. "You've got this thing for the past—or against the present. I'm never sure which."

"Maybe a little of both," I said. "I wish

Mencken would stop in. I'd like his opinion on the present.—What are you doing with it?"

"What?"

"The present. Here. Now."

"Oh." He spotted the waitress and ordered a beer. "Business trip," he said then. "To hire a consultant."

"Oh. How *is* business?"

"Complicated," he said, "complicated."

We lit cigarettes and after a while his beer arrived. We smoked and drank and listened to the music.

I've sung this song and I'll sing it again: the world is like an uptempoed piece of music. Of the many changes which came to pass during my lifetime, it seems that the majority have occurred during the past few years. It also struck me that way several years ago, and I'd a hunch I might be feeling the same way a few years hence—that is, if Don's business did not complicate me off this mortal coil or condenser before then.

Don operates the second-largest detective agency in the world, and he sometimes finds me useful because I do not exist. I do not exist now because I existed once at the time and the place where we attempted to begin scoring the wild ditty of our times. I refer to the world Central Data Bank project and the fact that I had had a significant part in that effort to construct a working model of the real world, accounting for everyone and everything in it. How well we succeeded and whether possession of the world's likeness does indeed provide its custodians with a greater measure of control over its functions, are questions my former colleagues still debate as the music grows more shrill and you can't see the maps for the pins. I made my decision back then and saw to it that I did not receive citizenship in that second world, a place which may now have become more important than the first. Exiled to reality, my own sojourns across the line are necessarily those of an alien guilty of illegal entry. I visit periodically because I go where I must to make my living.—That is where Don comes in. The people I can become are often very useful when he has peculiar problems.

Unfortunately, at that moment, it seemed that he did, just when the whole gang of me felt like turning down the volume and loafing.

We finished our drinks, got the bill, settled it.

"This way," I said, indicating the rear door, and he swung into his coat and followed me out.

"Talk here?" he asked, as we walked down the alley.

"Rather not," I said. "Public transportation, then private conversation."

He nodded and came along.

About three-quarters of an hour later we were in the saloon of the *Proteus* and I was making coffee. We were rocked gently by the Bay's chill waters, under a moonless sky. I'd only a pair of the smaller lights burning. Comfortable. On the water, aboard the *Proteus*, the crowding, the activities, the tempo, of life in the cities, on the land, are muted, slowed—fictionalized—by the metaphysical distancing a few meters of water can provide. We alter the landscape with great facility, but the ocean has always seemed unchanged, and I suppose by extension we are infected with some feelings of timelessness whenever we set out upon her. Maybe that's one of the reasons I spend so much time there.

"First time you've had me aboard," he said. "Comfortable. Very."

"Thanks.—Cream? Sugar?"

"Yes. Both."

We settled back with our steaming mugs and I asked, "What have you got?"

"One case involving two problems," he said. "One of them sort of falls within my area of competence. The other does not. I was told that it is an absolutely unique situation and would require the services of a very special specialist."

"I'm not a specialist at anything but keeping alive."

His eyes came up suddenly and caught my own.

"I had always assumed that you knew an awful lot about computers," he said.

I looked away. That was hitting below the belt. I had never held myself out to him as an authority in that area, and there had always been a tacit understanding between us that my methods of manipulating circumstance and identity were not open to discussion. On the other hand, it was obvious to him that my knowledge of the system was both extensive and intensive. Still, I didn't like talking about it. So I moved to defend.

"Computer people are a dime a dozen," I said. "It was probably different in your time, but these days they start teaching computer science to little kids their first year in school. So sure, I know a lot about it. This generation, everybody does."

"You know that is not what I meant," he said. "Haven't you known me long enough to trust me a little more than that? The question springs solely from the case at hand. That's all."

I nodded. Reactions by their very nature are not always appropriate, and I had invested a lot of emotional capital in a heavy-duty set. So, "Okay, I know more about them than the school kids," I said.

"Thanks. That can be our point of departure." He took a sip of coffee. "My own background is in law and accounting, followed by the military, military intelligence, and civil service, in that order. Then I got into this business. What technical stuff I know I've picked up along the way—a scrap here, a crash course there. I know a lot about what things can *do*, not so much about how they *work*. I did not understand the details on this one, so I want you to start at the top and explain things to me, for as far as you can go. I need the background review, and if you are able to furnish it I will also know that you are the man for the job. You can begin by telling me how the early space exploration robots worked—like, say the ones they used on Venus."

"That's not computers," I said, "and for that matter, they weren't really robots. They were telefactoring devices."

"Tell me what makes the difference."

"A robot is a machine which carries out certain operations in accordance with a program of instructions. A telefactor is a slave machine operated by remote control. The telefactor functions in a feedback situation with its operator. Depending on how sophisticated you want to get, the links can be audiovisual, kinesthetic, tactile, even olfactory. The more you want to go in this direction, the more anthropomorphic you get in the thing's design.

In the case of Venus, if I recall correctly, the human operator in orbit wore an exoskeleton which controlled the movements of the body, legs, arms, and hands of the device on the surface below, receiving motion and force feedback through a system of airjet transducers. He had on a helmet controlling the slave device's television camera—set, obviously enough, in its turret—which filled his field of vision with the scene below. He also wore earphones connected with its audio pickup. I read the book he wrote later. He said that for long stretches of time he would forget the cabin, forget that he was at the boss end of a control loop, and actually feel as if he were stalking through that hellish landscape. I remember being very impressed by it, just being a kid, and I wanted a super-tiny one all my own, so that I could wade around in puddles picking fights with microorganisms."

"Why?"

"Because there weren't any dragons on Venus. Anyhow, that is a telefactoring device, a thing quite distinct from a robot."

"I'm still with you," he said, and "Now tell me the difference between the early telefactoring devices and the later ones."

I swallowed some coffee.

"It was a bit trickier with respect to the outer planets and their satellites," I said. "There, we did not have orbiting operators at first. Economics, and some unresolved technical problems. Mainly economics. At any rate, the devices were landed on the target worlds, but the operators stayed home. Because of this, there was of course a time lag in the transmissions along the control loop. It took a while to receive the on-site input, and then there was another time lapse before the response movements reached the telefactor. We attempted to compensate for this in two ways: the first was by the employment of a simple wait-move, wait-move sequence; the second was more sophisticated and is actually the point where computers come into the picture in terms of participating in the control loop. It involved the setting up of models of known environmental factors, which were then enriched during the initial wait-move sequences. On this basis, the computer was then used to anticipate short-range developments. Finally, it could take over the loop and run it

by a combination of 'predictor controls' and
wait-move reviews. It still had to holler for human help, though, when unexpected things
came up. So, with the outer planets, it was neither totally automatic nor totally manual—nor
totally satisfactory—at first."

"Okay," he said, lighting a cigarette. "And the
next step?"

"The next wasn't really a technical step forward in telefactoring. It was an economic shift.
The pursestrings were loosened and we could
afford to send men out. We landed them where
we could land them, and in many of the places
where we could not, we sent down the telefactors and orbited the men again. Like in the old
days. The time-lag problem was removed because the operator was on top of things once
more. If anything, you can look at it as a rever-
sion to earlier methods. It is what we still often
do, though, and it works."

He shook his head.

"You left something out, between the computers and the bigger budget."

I shrugged.

"A number of things were tried during that
period, but none of them proved as effective as
what we already had going in the human-
computer partnership with the telefactors."

"There was one project," he said, "which attempted to get around the time-lag troubles by
sending the computer along with the telefactor
as part of the package. Only the computer

11

wasn't exactly a computer and the telefactor wasn't exactly a telefactor. Do you know which one I am referring to?"

I lit a cigarette of my own while I thought about it, then, "I think you are talking about the Hangman," I said.

"That's right, and this is where I get lost. Can you tell me how it works?"

"Ultimately, it was a failure," I said.

"But it worked at first."

"Apparently. But only on the easy stuff, on Io. It conked out later and had to be written off as a failure, albeit a noble one. The venture was overly ambitious from the very beginning. What seems to have happened was that the people in charge had the opportunity to combine vanguard projects—stuff that was still under investigation and stuff that was extremely new. In theory, it all seemed to dovetail so beautifully that they yielded to the temptation and incorporated too much. It started out well, but it fell apart later."

"But what all was involved in the thing?"

"Lord! What wasn't? The computer that wasn't exactly a computer . . . Okay, we'll start there. Last century, three engineers at the University of Wisconsin—Nordman, Parmentier, and Scott—developed a device known as a superconductive tunnel-junction neuristor. Two tiny strips of metal with a thin insulating layer between. Supercool it and it passed electrical impulses without resistance. Surround it with magnetized material and pack a mass of them together—billions—and what have you got?"

He shook his head.

"Well, for one thing you've got an impossible situation to schematize when considering all the paths and interconnections that may be formed. There is an obvious similarity to the structure of the brain. So, they theorized, you don't even attempt to hook up such a device. You pulse in data and let it establish its own preferential pathways, by means of the magnetic material's becoming increasingly magnetized each time the current passes through it, thus cutting the resistance. The material establishes its own routes in a fashion analogous to the functioning of the brain when it is learning something.

"In the case of the Hangman, they used a setup very similar to this and they were able to pack over ten billion neuristor-type cells into a very small area—around a cubic foot. They aimed for that magic figure because that is approximately the number of nerve cells in the human brain. That is what I meant when I said that it wasn't really a computer. They were actually working in the area of artificial intelligence, no matter what they called it."

"If the thing had its own brain—computer or quasihuman—then it was a robot rather than a telefactor, right?"

"Yes and no and maybe," I said. "It was operated as a telefactor device here on Earth—on the ocean floor, in the desert, in mountainous country—as part of its programming. I suppose you could also call that its apprenticeship—or kindergarten. Perhaps that is even more appropriate. It was being shown how to explore in difficult environments and to report back. Once it mastered this, then theoretically they could hang it out there in the sky without a control loop and let it report its own findings."

"At that point would it be considered a robot?"

"A robot is a machine which carries out certain operations in accordance with a program of instructions. The Hangman made its *own* decisions, you see. And I suspect that by trying to produce something that close to the human brain in structure and function, the seemingly inevitable randomness of its model got included in. It wasn't just a machine following a program. It was too complex. That was probably what broke it down."

Don chuckled.

"Inevitable free will?"

"No. As I said, they had thrown too many things into one bag. Everybody and his brother with a pet project that might be fitted in seemed a supersalesman that season. For example, the psychophysics boys had a gimmick they wanted to try on it, and it got used. Ostensibly, the Hangman was a communications device. Actually, they were concerned as to whether the thing was truly sentient."

"Was it?"

"Apparently so, in a limited fashion. What they had come up with, to be made part of the

14

initial telefactor loop, was a device which set up a weak induction field in the brain of the operator. The machine received and amplified the patterns of electrical activity being conducted in the Hangman's—might as well call it 'brain'—then passed them through a complex modulator and pulsed them into the induction field in the operator's head.—I am out of my area now and into that of Weber and Fechner, but a neuron has a threshold at which it will fire, and below which it will not. There are some forty thousand neurons packed together in a square millimeter of the cerebral cortex, in such a fashion that each one has several hundred synaptic connections with others about it. At any given moment, some of them may be way below the firing threshold while others are in a condition Sir John Eccles once referred to as 'critically poised'—ready to fire. If just one is pushed over the threshold, it can affect the discharge of hundreds of thousands of others within twenty milliseconds. The pulsating field was to provide such a push in a sufficiently selective fashion to give the operator an idea as to what was going on in the Hangman's brain. And vice versa. The Hangman was to have its own built-in version of the same thing. It was also thought that this might serve to humanize it somewhat, so that it would better appreciate the significance of its work—to instill something like loyalty, you might say."

"Do you think this could have contributed to its later breakdown?"

"Possibly. How can you say in a one-of-a-kind situation like this? If you want a guess, I'd say, 'Yes.' But it's just a guess."

"Uh-huh," he said, "and what were its physical capabilities?"

"Anthropomorphic design," I said, "both because it was originally telefactored and because of the psychological reasoning I just mentioned. It could pilot its own small vessel. No need for a life-support system, of course. Both it and the vessel were powered by fusion units, so that fuel was no real problem. Self-repairing. Capable of performing a great variety of sophisticated tests and measurements, of making observations, completing reports, learning new material, broadcasting its findings back here. Capable of surviving just about anywhere. In fact, it required less energy on the outer planets—less work for the refrigeration units, to maintain that supercooled brain in its midsection."

"How strong was it?"

"I don't recall all the specs. Maybe a dozen times as strong as a man, in things like lifting and pushing."

"It explored Io for us and started in on Europa."

"Yes."

"Then it began behaving erratically, just when we thought it had really learned its job."

"That sounds right," I said.

"It refused a direct order to explore Callisto, then headed out toward Uranus."

16

"Yes. It's been years since I read the reports. . . ."

"The malfunction worsened after that. Long periods of silence interspersed with garbled transmissions. Now that I know more about its makeup, it almost sounds like a man going off the deep end."

"It seems similar."

"But it managed to pull itself together again for a brief while. It landed on Titania, began sending back what seemed like appropriate observation reports. This only lasted a short time, though. It went irrational once more, indicated that it was heading for a landing on Uranus itself, and that was it. We didn't hear from it after that. Now that I know about that mind-reading gadget I understand why a psychiatrist on this end could be so positive it would never function again."

"I never heard about that part."

"I did."

I shrugged. "This was all around twenty years ago," I said, "and, as I mentioned, it has been a long while since I've read anything about it."

"The Hangman's ship crashed or landed, as the case may be, in the Gulf of Mexico, two days ago."

I just stared at him.

"It was empty," Don went on, "when they finally got out and down to it."

"I don't understand."

"Yesterday morning," he continued, "restaurateur Manny Burns was found beaten to death in the office of his establishment, the Maison Saint-Michel, in New Orleans."

"I still fail to see—"

"Manny Burns was one of the four original operators who programmed—pardon me, 'taught'—the Hangman."

The silence lengthened, dragged its belly on the deck.

"Coincidence . . . ?" I finally said.

"My client doesn't think so."

"Who is your client?"

"One of the three remaining members of the training group. He is convinced that the Hangman has returned to Earth to kill its former operators."

"Has he made his fears known to his old employers?"

"No."

"Why not?"

"Because it would require telling them the reason for his fears."

"That being . . . ?"

"He wouldn't tell me, either."

"How does he expect you to do a proper job?"

"He told me what he considered a proper job. He wants two things done, neither of which requires a full case history. He wanted to be furnished with good bodyguards, and he wanted the Hangman found and disposed of. I have already taken care of the first part."

"And you want me to do the second?"

18

"That's right. You have confirmed my opinion that you are the man for the job."

"I see. Do you realize that if the thing is truly sentient this will be something very like murder? If it is not, of course, then it will only amount to the destruction of expensive government property."

"Which way do you look at it?"

"I look at it as a job," I said.

"You'll take it?"

"I need more facts before I can decide. Like who is your client? Who are the other operators? Where do they live? What do they do? What—"

He raised his hand.

"First," he said, "the Honorable Jesse Brockden, senior Senator from Wisconsin, is our client. Confidentiality, of course, is written all over it."

I nodded. "I remember his being involved with the space program before he went into politics. I wasn't aware of the specifics, though. He could get government protection so easily—"

"To obtain it, he would apparently have to tell them something he doesn't want to talk about. Perhaps it would hurt his career. I simply do not know. He doesn't want them. He wants us."

I nodded again.

"What about the others? Do they want us, too?"

"Quite the opposite. They don't subscribe to

Brockden's notions at all. They seem to think he is something of a paranoid."

"How well do they know one another these days?"

"They live in different parts of the country, haven't seen each other in years. Been in occasional touch, though."

"Kind of flimsy basis for that diagnosis, then."

"One of them *is* a psychiatrist."

"Oh. Which one?"

"Leila Thackery is her name. Lives in St. Louis. Works at the State Hospital there."

"None of them have gone to any authority, then—federal or local?"

"That's right. Brockden contacted them when he heard about the Hangman. He was in Washington at the time. Got word on its return right away and managed to get the story killed. He tried to reach them all, learned about Burns in the process, contacted me, then tried to persuade the others to accept protection by my people. They weren't buying. When I talked to her, Doctor Thackery pointed out—quite correctly—that Brockden is a very sick man."

"What's he got?"

"Cancer. In his spine. Nothing they can do about it once it hits there and digs in. He even told me he figures he has maybe six months to get through what he considers a very important piece of legislation—the new criminal rehabilitation act.—I will admit that he did sound kind of paranoid when he talked about it. But hell!

Who wouldn't? Dr. Thackery sees that as the whole thing, though, and she doesn't see the Burns killing as being connected with the Hangman. Thinks it was just a traditional robbery gone sour, thief surprised and panicky, maybe hopped-up, *et cetera*."

"Then she is not afraid of the Hangman?"

"She said that she is in a better position to know its mind than anyone else, and she is not especially concerned."

"What about the other operator?"

"He said that Doctor Thackery may know its mind better than anyone else, but he knows its brain, and he isn't worried, either."

"What did he mean by that?"

"David Fentris is a consulting engineer— electronics, cybernetics. He actually had something to do with the Hangman's design."

I got to my feet and went after the coffeepot. Not that I'd an overwhelming desire for another cup at just that moment. But I had known, had once worked with a David Fentris. And he had at one time been connected with the space program.

About fifteen years my senior, Dave had been with the Data Bank project when I had known him. Where a number of us had begun having second thoughts as the thing progressed, Dave had never been anything less than wildly enthusiastic. A wiry five-eight, gray-cropped, gray eyes back of hornrims and heavy glass, cycling between preoccupation and near-frantic darting, he had had a way of verbalizing half-completed thoughts as he went along, so that you might begin to think him a representative of that tribe which had come into positions of small authority by means of nepotism or politics. If you would listen a few more minutes, however, you would begin revising your opinion as he started to pull his musings together into a rigorous framework. By the time he had finished, you generally wondered why you hadn't seen it all along and what a guy like that was doing in a position of such small authority. Later, it might strike you, though, that he seemed sad whenever he wasn't enthusiastic about something. And while the gung-ho spirit is great for short-range projects, larger ventures generally require somewhat more equanimity. I wasn't at all surprised that he had wound up as a consultant.

The big question now, of course was: Would he remember me? True, my appearance was altered, my personality hopefully more mature, my habits shifted around. But would that be enough, should I have to encounter him as part of this job? That mind behind those hornrims could do a lot of strange things with just a little data.

"Where does he live?" I asked.

"Memphis.—And what's the matter?"

"Just trying to get my geography straight," I said. "Is Senator Brockden still in Washington?"

"No. He's returned to Wisconsin and is currently holed up in a lodge in the northern part of the state. Four of my people are with him."

"I see."

I refreshed our coffee supply and reseated myself. I didn't like this one at all and I resolved not to take it. I didn't like just giving Don a flat "No," though. His assignments had become a very important part of my life, and this one was not mere legwork. It was obviously important to him, and he wanted me on it. I decided to look for holes in the thing, to find some way of reducing it to the simple bodyguard job already in progress.

"It does seem peculiar," I said, "that Brockden is the only one afraid of the device."

"Yes."

". . . And that he gives no reasons."

"True."

". . . Plus his condition, and what the doctor said about its effect on his mind."

"I have no doubt that he is neurotic," Don said. "Look at this."

He reached for his coat, withdrew a sheaf of papers from within it. He shuffled through them and extracted a single sheet, which he passed to me.

It was a piece of Congressional-letterhead stationery, with the message scrawled in longhand: *"Don,"* it said, *"I've got to see you. Frankenstein's monster is just come back from where we hung him and he's looking for me. The whole damn universe is trying to grind me up. Call me between 8 & 10.—Jess."*

I nodded, started to pass it back, paused, then handed it over. Double damn it deeper than hell!

I took a drink of coffee. I thought that I had

long ago given up hope in such things, but I had noticed something which immediately troubled me. In the margin, where they list such matters, I had seen that Jesse Brockden was on the committee for review of the Central Data Bank program. I recalled that that committee was supposed to be working on a series of reform recommendations. Offhand, I could not remember Brockden's position on any of the issues involved, but—Oh hell! The thing was simply too big to alter significantly now. . . . But it *was* the only real Frankenstein monster I cared about, and there was always the possibility. . . . On the other hand—Hell, again! What if I let him die when I might have saved him, and he had been the one who . . . ?

I took another drink of coffee. I lit another cigarette.

There might be a way of working it so that Dave didn't even come into the picture. I could talk to Leila Thackery first, check further into the Burns killing, keep posted on new developments, find out more about the vessel in the Gulf. . . . I might be able to accomplish something, even if it was only the negation of Brockden's theory, without Dave's and my paths ever crossing.

"Have you got the specs on the Hangman?" I asked.

"Right here."

He passed them over.

"The police report on the Burns killing?"

"Here it is."

"The whereabouts of everyone involved, and some background on them?"

"Here."

"The place or places where I can reach you during the next few days—around the clock? This one may require some coordination."

He smiled and reached for his pen.

"Glad to have you aboard," he said.

I reached over and tapped the barometer. I shook my head.

The ringing of the phone awakened me. Reflex bore me across the room, where I took it on audio.

"Yes?"

"Mr. Donne? It is eight o'clock."

"Thanks."

I collapsed into the chair. I am what might be called a slow starter. I tend to recapitulate phylogeny every morning. Basic desires inched their ways through my gray matter to close a connection. Slowly, I extended a cold-blooded member and clicked my talons against a couple of numbers. I croaked my desire for food and lots of coffee to the voice that responded. Half an hour later I would only have growled. Then I staggered off to the place of flowing waters to renew my contact with basics.

In addition to my normal adrenaline and blood-sugar bearishness, I had not slept much the night before. I had closed up shop after Don left, stuffed my pockets with essentials, departed the *Proteus*, gotten myself over to the airport and onto a flight which took me to St. Louis in the dead, small hours of the dark. I was unable to sleep during the flight, thinking about the case, deciding on the tack I was going to take with Leila Thackery. On arrival, I had checked into the airport motel, left a message to be awakened at an unreasonable hour, and collapsed.

As I ate, I regarded the fact sheet Don had given me.

Leila Thackery was currently single, having divorced her second husband a little over two years ago, was forty-six years old, and lived in an apartment near to the hospital where she worked. Attached to the sheet was a photo which might have been ten years old. In it, she was brunette, light-eyed, barely on the right side of that border between ample and overweight, with fancy glasses straddling an upturned nose. She had published a number of books and articles with titles full of alienations, roles, transactions, social contexts, and more alienations.

I hadn't had the time to go my usual route, becoming an entire new individual with a verifiable history. Just a name and a story, that's all. It did not seem necessary this time, though. For once, something approximating honesty actually seemed a reasonable approach.

I took a public vehicle over to her apartment building. I did not phone ahead, because it is easier to say "No" to a voice than to a person.

According to the record, today was one of the days when she saw outpatients in her home. Her idea, apparently: break down the alienating in-stitution-image, remove resentments by turning the sessions into something more like social oc-casions, *et cetera*. I did not want all that much of her time—I had decided that Don could make it worth her while if it came to that—and I was sure my fellows' visits were scheduled to leave her with some small breathing space. *Inter alia*, so to speak.

I had just located her name and apartment number amid the buttons in the entrance foyer when an old woman passed behind me and un-locked the door to the lobby. She glanced at me and held it open, so I went on in without ring-ing. The matter of presence, again.

took the elevator to Leila's floor, the second, located her door and knocked on it. I was al-most ready to knock again when it opened, part-way.

"Yes?" she asked, and I revised my estimate as to the age of the photo. She looked just about the same.

"Doctor Thackery," I said, "my name is Donne. You could help me quite a bit with a problem I've got."

"What sort of problem?"

"It involves a device known as the Hangman."

She sighed and showed me a quick grimace. Her fingers tightened on the door.

"I've come a long way but I'll be easy to get rid of. I've only a few things I'd like to ask you about it."

"Are you with the government?"

"No."

"Do you work for Brockden?"

"No, I'm something different."

"All right," she said. "Right now I've got a group session going. It will probably last around another half hour. If you don't mind waiting down in the lobby, I'll let you know as soon as it is over. We can talk then."

"Good enough," I said. "Thanks."

She nodded, closed the door. I located the stairway and walked back down.

A cigarette later, I decided that the devil finds work for idle hands and thanked him for his suggestion. I strolled back toward the foyer. Through the glass, I read the names of a few residents of the fifth floor. I elevated up and knocked on one of the doors. Before it was opened I had my notebook and pad in plain sight.

"Yes?" Short, fiftyish, curious.

"My name is Stephen Foster, Mrs. Gluntz. I am doing a survey for the North American Consumers League. I would like to pay you for a couple minutes of your time, to answer some questions about products you use."

"Why—Pay me?"

"Yes, ma'am. Ten dollars. Around a dozen questions. It will just take a minute or two."

"All right." She opened the door wider. "Won't you come in?"

"No, thank you. This thing is so brief I'd just be in and out. The first question involves detergents . . ."

Ten minutes later I was back in the lobby adding the thirty bucks for the three interviews to the list of expenses I was keeping. When a situation is full of unpredictables and I am playing makeshift games, I like to provide for as many contingencies as I can.

Another quarter of an hour or so slipped by before the elevator opened and discharged three guys—young, young, and middle-aged, casually dressed, chuckling over something.

The big one on the nearest end strolled over and nodded.

"You the fellow waiting to see Dr. Thackery?"

"That's right."

"She said to tell you to come on up now."

"Thanks."

I rode up again, returned to her door. She opened to my knock, nodded me in, saw me seated in a comfortable chair at the far end of her living room.

"Would you care for a cup of coffee?" she asked. "It's fresh. I made more than I needed."

"That would be fine. Thanks."

Moments later, she brought in a couple of cups, delivered one to me, and seated herself on the sofa to my left. I ignored the cream and sugar on the tray and took a sip.

"You've gotten me interested," she said. "Tell me about it."

"Okay, I have been told that the telefactor device known as the Hangman, now possibly possessed of an artificial intelligence, has returned to Earth—"

"Hypothetical," she said, "unless you know something I don't. I have been told that the Hangman's vehicle reentered and crashed in the Gulf. There is no evidence that the vehicle was occupied."

"It seems a reasonable conclusion, though."

"It seems just as reasonable to me that the Hangman sent the vehicle off toward an eventual rendezvous point many years ago and that it only recently reached that point, at which time the reentry program took over and brought it down."

"Why should it return the vehicle and strand itself out there?"

"Before I answer that," she said, "I would like to know the reason for your concern. News media?"

"No," I said. "I am a science writer—straight tech, popular, and anything in between. But I am not after a piece for publication. I was retained to do a report on the psychological make-up of the thing."

"For whom?"

"A private investigation outfit. They want to know what might influence its thinking, how it might be likely to behave—if it has indeed come back.—I've been doing a lot of homework, and I gathered there is a likelihood that its nuclear personality was a composite of the minds of its four operators. So, personal contacts seemed in order, to collect your opinions as to what it might be like. I came to you first for obvious reasons."

She nodded.

"A Mister Walsh spoke with me the other day. He is working for Senator Brockden."

"Oh? I never go into an employer's business beyond what he's asked me to do. Senator Brockden is on my list though, along with a David Fentris."

"You were told about Manny Burns?"

"Yes. Unfortunate."

"That is apparently what set Jesse off. He is—how shall I put it?—he is clinging to life right now, trying to accomplish a great many things in the time he has remaining. Every moment is precious to him. He feels the old man in the white nightgown breathing down his neck.— Then the ship returns and one of us is killed. From what we know of the Hangman, the last we heard of it, it had become irrational. Jesse saw a connection, and in his condition the fear is understandable. There is nothing wrong with humoring him if it allows him to get his work done."

"But you don't see a threat in it?"

"No. I was the last person to monitor the Hangman before communications ceased, and I could see then what had happened. The first things that it had learned were the organization of perceptions and motor activities. Multitudes of other patterns had been transferred from the minds of its operators, but they were too sophisticated to mean much initially.—Think of a child who has learned the Gettysburg Address. It is there in his head, that is all. One day, however, it may be important to him. Conceivably, it may even inspire him to action. It takes some growing up first, of course. Now think of such a child with a great number of conflicting patterns—attitudes, tendencies, memories—none of which are especially bothersome for so long as he remains a child. Add a bit of maturity, though—and bear in mind that the patterns originated with four different individuals, all of them more powerful than the words of even the finest of speeches, bearing as they do their own built-in feelings. Try to imagine the conflicts, the contradictions involved in being four people at once—"

"Why wasn't this imagined in advance?" I asked.

"Ah!" she said, smiling. "The full sensitivity of the neuristor brain was not appreciated at first. It was assumed that the operators were adding data in a linear fashion and that this would continue until a critical mass was achieved, corresponding to the construction of a model or picture of the world which would then serve as a point of departure for growth of the Hangman's own mind. And it did seem to check out this way.

"What actually occurred, however, was a phenomenon amounting to imprinting. Secondary characteristics of the operators' minds, outside the didactic situations, were imposed. These did not immediately become functional and hence were not detected. They remained latent until the mind had developed sufficiently to understand them. And then it was too late. It suddenly acquired four additional personalities and was unable to coordinate them. When it tried to compartmentalize them it went schizoid; when it tried to integrate them it went catatonic. It was cycling back and forth between these alternatives at the end. Then it just went silent. I felt it had undergone the equivalent of an epileptic seizure. Wild currents through that magnetic material would, in effect, have erased its mind, resulting in *its* equivalent of death or idiocy."

"I follow you," I said. "Now, just for the sake of playing games, I see the alternatives as either a successful integration of all this material or the achievement of a viable schizophrenia. What do you think its behavior would be like if either of these were possible?"

"All right," she agreed. "As I just said, though, I think there were physical limitations to its retaining multiple personality structures for a very long period of time. If it did, however, it would have continued with its own, plus replicas of the four operators', at least for a while. The situation would differ radically from that of a human schizoid of this sort, in that the additional personalities were valid images of genuine identities rather than self-generated complexes which had become autonomous. They might continue to evolve, they might degenerate, they might conflict to the point of destruction or gross modification of any or all of them. In other words, no prediction is possible as to the nature of whatever might remain."

33

"Might I venture one?"

"Go ahead."

"After considerable anxiety, it masters them. It asserts itself. It beats down this quartet of demons which has been tearing it apart, acquiring in the process an all-consuming hatred for the actual individuals responsible for this turmoil. To free itself totally, to revenge itself, to work its ultimate catharsis, it resolves to seek them out and destroy them."

She smiled.

"You have just dispensed with the 'viable schizophrenia' you conjured up, and you have now switched over to its pulling through and becoming fully autonomous. That is a different situation—no matter what strings you put on it."

"OK, I accept the charge.—But what about my conclusion?"

"You are saying that if it did pull through, it would hate us. That strikes me as an unfair attempt to invoke the spirit of Sigmund Freud: Oedipus and Electra in one being, out to destroy all its parents—the authors of every one of its tensions, anxieties, hang-ups, burned into its impressionable psyche at a young and defenseless age. Even Freud didn't have a name for that one. What should we call it?"

"A Hermacis complex?" I suggested.

"Hermacis?"

"Hermaphroditus having been united in one body with the nymph Salmacis, I've just done the same with their names. That being would

34

then have had four parents against whom to react."

"Cute," she said, smiling. "If the liberal arts do nothing else, they provide engaging metaphors for the thinking they displace. This one is unwarranted and overly anthropomorphic, though.—You wanted my opinion. All right. If the Hangman pulled through at all, it could only have been by virtue of that neuristor brain's differences from the human brain. From my own professional experience, a human could not pass through a situation like that and attain stability. If the Hangman did, it would have to have resolved all the contradictions and conflicts, to have mastered and understood the situation so thoroughly that I do not believe whatever remained could involve that sort of hatred. The fear, the uncertainty, the things that feed hate would have been analyzed, digested, turned to something more useful. There would probably be distaste, and possibly an act of independence, of self-assertion. That was one reason why I suggested its return of the ship."

"It is your opinion, then, that if the Hangman exists as a thinking individual today, this is the only possible attitude it would possess toward its former operators: it would want nothing more to do with you?"

"That is correct. Sorry about your Hermacis complex. But in this case we must look to the brain, not the psyche. And we see two things: schizophrenia would have destroyed it, and a successful resolution of its problem would preclude vengeance. Either way, there is nothing to worry about."

How could I put it tactfully? I decided that I could not.

"All of this is fine," I said, "for as far as it goes. But getting away from both the purely psychological and the purely physical, could there be a particular reason for its seeking your deaths—that is, a plain old-fashioned motive for a killing, based on *events* rather than having to do with the way its thinking equipment goes together?"

Her expression was impossible to read, but considering her line of work I had expected nothing less.

"What events?" she said.

"I have no idea. That's why I asked."

She shook her head.

"I'm afraid that I don't, either."

"Then that about does it," I said. "I can't think of anything else to ask you."

She nodded.

"And I can't think of anything else to tell you."

I finished my coffee, returned the cup to the tray.

"Thanks, then," I said, "for your time, for the coffee. You have been very helpful."

I rose. She did the same.

"What are you going to do now?" she asked.

"I haven't quite decided," I answered. "I want to do the best report I can. Have you any suggestions on that?"

"I suggest that there isn't any more to learn, that I have given you the only possible constructions the facts warrant."

"You don't feel David Fentris could provide any additional insights?"

She snorted, then sighed.

"No," she said, "I do not think he could tell you anything useful."

"What do you mean? From the way you say it—"

"I know. I didn't mean to.—Some people find comfort in religion. Others . . . You know. Others take it up late in life with a vengeance and a half. They don't use it quite the way it was intended. It comes to color all their thinking."

"Fanaticism?" I said.

"Not exactly. A misplaced zeal. A masochistic sort of thing. Hell! I shouldn't be diagnosing at a distance—or influencing your opinion. Forget what I said. Form your own opinion when you meet him."

She raised her head, appraising my reaction.

"Well," I responded, "I am not at all certain that I am going to see him. But you have made me curious. How can religion influence engineering?"

"I spoke with him after Jesse gave us the news on the vessel's return. I got the impression at the time that he feels we were tampering in the province of the Almighty by attempting the creation of an artificial intelligence. That our creation should go mad was only appropriate, being the work of imperfect man. He seemed to feel that it would be fitting if it had come back for retribution, as a sign of judgment upon us."

"Oh," I said.

She smiled then. I returned it.

"Yes," she said, "but maybe I just got him in a bad mood. Maybe you should go see for yourself."

Something told me to shake my head—there was a bit of a difference between this view of him, my recollections, and Don's comment that Dave had said he knew its brain and was not especially concerned. Somewhere among these lay something I felt I should know, felt I should learn without seeming to pursue.

So, "I think I have enough right now," I said. "It was the psychological side of things I was supposed to cover, not the mechanical—*or* the theological. You have been extremely helpful. Thanks again."

She carried her smile all the way to the door.

"If it is not too much trouble," she said, as I stepped into the hall, "I would like to learn how this whole thing finally turns out—or any interesting developments, for that matter."

"My connection with the case ends with this report, and I am going to write it now. Still, I may get some feedback."

"You have my number . . . ?"

"Probably, but . . ."

I already had it, but I jotted it again, right after Mrs. Gluntz's answers to my inquiries on detergents.

* * *

38

Moving in a rigorous line, I made beautiful connections, for a change. I headed directly for the airport, found a flight aimed at Memphis, bought passage and was the last to board. Ten-score seconds, perhaps, made all the difference. Not even a tick or two to spare for checking out of the motel.—No matter. The good head doctor had convinced me that, like it or not, David Fentris was next, damn it. I had too strong a feeling that Leila Thackery had not told me the entire story. I had to take a chance, to see these changes in the man for myself, to try to figure out how they related to the Hangman. For a number of reasons, I'd a feeling they might.

I disembarked into a cool, partly overcast afternoon, found transportation almost immediately and set out for Dave's office address.

A before-the-storm feeling came over me as I entered and crossed the town. A dark wall of clouds continued to build in the west. Later, standing before the building where Dave did business, the first few drops of rain were already spattering against its dirty brick front. It would take a lot more than that to freshen it, though, or any of the others in the area. I would have thought he'd have come a little further than this by now.

I shrugged off some moisture and went inside.

The directory gave me directions, the elevator elevated me, my feet found the way to his door. I knocked on it. After a time, I knocked

again and waited again. Again, nothing. So I
tried it, found it open, and went on in.

It was a small, vacant waiting room, green-
carpeted. The reception desk was dusty. I
crossed and peered around the plastic partition
behind it.

The man had his back to me. I drummed my
knuckles against the partitioning. He heard it
and turned.

"Yes?"

Our eyes met, his still framed by hornrims
and just as active; lenses thicker, hair thinner,
cheeks a trifle hollower.

His question mark quivered in the air, and
nothing in his gaze moved to replace it with recognition. He had been bending over a sheaf of
schematics. A lopsided basket of metal, quartz,
porcelain, and glass rested on a nearby table.

"My name is Donne, John Donne," I said. "I
am looking for David Fentris."

"I am David Fentris."

"Good to meet you," I said, crossing to where
he stood. "I am assisting in an investigation
concerning a project with which you were once
associated . . ."

He smiled and nodded, accepted my hand and
shook it.

"The Hangman, of course. Glad to know you,
Mister Donne."

"Yes, the Hangman," I said. "I am doing a
report—"

"—And you want my opinion as to how dangerous it is. Sit down." He gestured toward a

40

chair at the end of his work bench. "Care for a cup of tea?"

"No, thanks."

"I'm having one."

"Well, in that case . . ."

He crossed to another bench.

"No cream. Sorry."

"That's all right.—How did you know it involved the Hangman?"

He grinned as he brought me my cup.

"Because it's come back," he said, "and it's the only thing I've been connected with that warrants that much concern."

"Do you mind talking about it?"

"Up to a point, no."

"What's the point?"

"If we get near it, I'll let you know."

"Fair enough.—How dangerous *is* it?"

"I would say that it is harmless," he replied, "except to three persons."

"Formerly four?"

"Precisely."

"How come?"

"We were doing something we had no business doing."

"That being . . . ?"

"For one thing, attempting to create an artificial intelligence."

"Why had you no business doing that?"

"A man with a name like yours shouldn't have to ask."

I chuckled.

"If I were a preacher," I said, "I would have

to point out that there is no biblical injunction against it—unless you've been worshiping it on the sly."

He shook his head.

"Nothing that simple, that obvious, that explicit. Times have changed since the Good Book was written, and you can't hold with a purely fundamentalist approach in complex times. What I was getting at was something a little more abstract. A form of pride, not unlike the classical hubris—the setting up of oneself on a level with the Creator."

"Did you feel that—pride?"

"Yes."

"Are you sure it wasn't just enthusiasm for an ambitious project that was working well?"

"Oh, there was plenty of that. A manifestation of the same thing."

"I do seem to recall something about man being made in the Creator's image, and something else about trying to live up to that. It would seem to follow that exercising one's capacities along similar lines would be a step in the right direction—an act of conformance with the Divine ideal, if you'd like."

"But I don't like. Man cannot really create. He can only rearrange what is already present. Only God can create."

"Then you have nothing to worry about."

He frowned. Then, "No," he said. "Being aware of this and still trying is where the presumption comes in."

"Were you really thinking that way when you

did it? Or did all this occur to you after the fact?"

He continued to frown.

"I am no longer certain."

"Then it would seem to me that a merciful God would be inclined to give you the benefit of the doubt."

He gave me a wry smile.

"Not bad, John Donne. But I feel that judgment may already have been entered and that we may have lost four to nothing."

"Then you see the Hangman as an avenging angel?"

"Sometimes. Sort of. I see it as being returned to exact a penalty."

"Just for the record," I suggested, "if the Hangman had had full access to the necessary equipment and was able to construct another unit such as itself, would you consider it guilty of the same thing that is bothering you?"

He shook his head.

"Don't get all cute and jesuitical with me, Donne. I'm not that far away from fundamentals. Besides, I'm willing to admit I might be wrong and that there may be other forces driving it to the same end."

"Such as?"

"I told you I'd let you know when we reached a certain point. That's it."

"Okay," I said. "But that sort of blank-walls me, you know. The people I am working for would like to protect you people. They want to stop the Hangman. I was hoping you would tell me a little more—if not for your own sake, then for the others'. They might not share your philosophical sentiments, and you have just admitted you may be wrong.—Despair, by the way, is also considered a sin by a great number of theologians."

He sighed and stroked his nose, as I had often seen him do in times long past.

"What do you do, anyhow?" he asked me.

"Me, personally? I'm a science writer. I'm putting together a report on the device for the agency that wants to do the protecting. The better my report, the better their chances."

He was silent for a time, then, "I read a lot in the area, but I don't recognize your name," he said.

"Most of my work has involved petrochemistry and marine biology," I said.

"Oh.—You were a peculiar choice then, weren't you?"

"Not really. I was available, and the boss knows my work, knows I'm good."

He glanced across the room, to where a stack of cartons partly obscured what I then realized to be a remote-access terminal. Okay. If he decided to check out my credentials now, John Donne would fall apart. It seemed a hell of a time to get curious, though, *after* sharing his sense of sin with me. He must have thought so, too, because he did not look that way again.

"Let me put it this way . . ." he finally said, and something of the old David Fentris at his best took control of his voice. "For one reason or the other, I believe that it wants to destroy its former operators. If it is the judgment of the Almighty, that's all there is to it. It will succeed. If not, however, I don't want any outside protection. I've done my own repenting and it is up to me to handle the rest of the situation myself, too. I will stop the Hangman personally—right here—before anyone else is hurt."

"How?" I asked him.

He nodded toward the glittering helmet.

"With that," he said.

"How?" I repeated.

"The Hangman's telefactor circuits are still intact. They have to be. They are an integral part of it. It could not disconnect them without shutting itself down. If it comes within a quarter mile of here, that unit will be activated. It will emit a loud humming sound and a light will begin to blink behind that meshing beneath the forward ridge. I will then don the helmet and take control of the Hangman. I will bring it here and disconnect its brain."

"How would you do the disconnect?"

He reached for the schematics he had been looking at when I had come in.

"Here. The thoracic plate has to be unplugged. There are four subunits that have to be uncoupled. Here, here, here, and here."

He looked up.

"You would have to do them in sequence, though, or it could get mighty hot," I said. "First this one, then these two. Then the other."

When I looked up again, the gray eyes were fixed on my own.

"I thought you were in petrochemistry and marine biology," he said.

"I am not really 'in' anything," I said. "I am a tech writer, with bits and pieces from all over—and I did have a look at these before, when I accepted the job."

"I see."

"Why don't you bring the space agency in on this?" I said, working to shift ground. "The original telefactoring equipment had all that power and range—"

"It was dismantled a long time ago.—I thought you were with the Government."

I shook my head.

"Sorry. I didn't mean to mislead you. I am on contract with a private investigation outfit."

"Uh-huh. Then that means Jesse.—Not that it matters. You can tell him that one way or the other everything is being taken care of."

"What if you are wrong on the supernatural," I said, "but correct on the other? Supposing it is coming under the circumstances you feel it proper to resist? But supposing you are not next on its list? Supposing it gets to one of the others next, instead of you? If you are so sensitive about guilt and sin, don't you think that you would be responsible for that death—if you could prevent it by telling me just a little bit more? If it's confidentiality you're worried about—"

"No," he said. "You cannot trick me into applying my principles to a hypothetical situation which will only work out the way that you want it to. Not when I am certain that it will not arise. Whatever moves the Hangman, it will come to *me* next. If I cannot stop it, then it cannot be stopped until it has completed its job."

"How do you know that you are next?"

"Take a look at a map," he said. "It landed in the Gulf. Manny was right there in New Orleans. Naturally, he was first. The Hangman can move underwater like a controlled torpedo, which makes the Mississippi its logical route for inconspicuous travel. Proceeding up it then, here I am in Memphis. Then Leila, up in St. Louis, is obviously next after me. It can worry about getting to Washington after that."

I thought about Senator Brockden in Wisconsin and decided it would not even have that problem. All of them were fairly accessible, when you thought of the situation in terms of river travel.

"But how is it to know where you all are?" I asked.

"Good question," he said. "Within a limited range, it was once sensitive to our brain waves, having an intimate knowledge of them and the ability to pick them up. I do not know what that range would be today. It might have been able to construct an amplifier to extend this area of perception. But to be more mundane about it, I believe that it simply consulted Central's national directory. There are booths all over, even on the waterfront. It could have hit one late at night and gimmicked it. It certainly had sufficient identifying information—and engineering skill."

"Then it seems to me thatthe best bet for all

of you would be to move away from the river till this business is settled. That thing won't be able to stalk about the countryside very long without being noticed."

He shook his head.

"It would find a way. It is extremely resourceful. At night, in an overcoat, a hat, it could pass. It requires nothing that a man would need. It could dig a hole and bury itself, stay underground during daylight. It could run without resting all night long. There is no place it could not reach in a surprisingly short while.—No, I must wait here for it."

"Let me put it as bluntly as I can," I said. "If you are right that it is a Divine Avenger, I would say that it smacks of blasphemy to try to tackle it. On the other hand, if it is not, then I think you are guilty of jeopardizing the others by withholding information that would allow us to provide them with a lot more protection than you are capable of giving them all by yourself."

He laughed.

"I'll just have to learn to live with that guilt, too, as they do with theirs," he said. "After I've done my best, they deserve anything they get."

"It was my understanding," I said, "that even God doesn't judge people until after they're dead—if you want another piece of presumption to add to your collection."

He stopped laughing and studied my face.

"There is something familiar about the way you talk, the way you think," he said. "Have we ever met before?"

"I doubt it. I would have remembered."

He shook his head.

"You've got a way of bothering a man's thinking that rings a faint bell," he went on. "You trouble me, sir."

"That was my intention."

"Are you staying here in town?"

"No."

"Give me a number where I can reach you, will you? If I have any new thoughts on this thing, I'll call you."

"I wish you would have them now, if you are going to have them."

"No, I've got some thinking to do. Where can I get hold of you later?"

I gave him the name of the motel I was still checked into in St. Louis. I could call back periodically for messages.

"All right," he said, and he moved toward the partition by the reception area and stood beside it.

I rose and followed him, passing into that area and pausing at the door to the hall.

"One thing . . ." I said.

"Yes?"

"If it does show up and you do stop it, will you call me and tell me that?"

"Yes, I will."

"Thanks then—and good luck."

Impulsively, I extended my hand. He gripped it and smiled faintly.

"Thank you, Mr. Donne."

* * *

Next. Next, next, next . . .

I couldn't budge Dave, and Leila Thackery had given me everything she was going to. No real sense in calling Don yet—not until I had more to say.

I thought it over on my way back to the airport. The pre-dinner hours always seem best for talking to people in any sort of official capacity, just as the night seems best for dirty work. Heavily psychological, but true nevertheless. I hated to waste the rest of the day if there was anyone else worth talking to before I called Don. Going through the folder, I decided that there was.

Manny Burns had a brother, Phil. I wondered how worthwhile it might be to talk with him. I could make it to New Orleans at a sufficiently respectable hour, learn whatever he was willing to tell me, check back with Don for new developments, and then decide whether there was anything I should be about with respect to the vessel itself.

The sky was gray and leaky above me. I was anxious to flee its spaces. So I decided to do it. I could think of no better stone to upturn at the moment.

At the airport, I was ticketed quickly, in time for another close connection.

Hurrying to reach my flight, my eyes brushed over a half-familiar face on the passing escalator. The reflex reserved for such occasions seemed to catch us both, because he looked back, too, with the same eyebrow twitch of startle and scrutiny.

Then he was gone. I could not place him, however. The half-familiar face becomes a familiar phenomenon in a crowded, highly mobile society. I sometimes think that this is all that will eventually remain of any of us: patterns of features, some a trifle more persistent than others, impressed on the flow of bodies. A small-town boy in a big city. Thomas Wolfe must long ago have felt the same thing when he had coined the word "manswarm." It might have been someone I'd once met briefly, or simply someone—or someone like someone—I had passed on sufficient other occasions such as this.

As I flew the unfriendly skies out of Memphis, I mulled over musings past on artificial intelligence, or AI as they have tagged it in the think-box biz. When talking about computers, the AI notion had always seemed hotter than I deemed necessary, partly because of semantics. The word "intelligence" has all sorts of tag-along associations of the non-physical sort. I suppose it goes back to the fact that early discussions and conjectures concerning it made it sound as if the potential for intelligence was always present in the array of gadgets, and that the correct procedures, the right programs, simply had to be found to call it forth. When you looked at it that way, as many did, it gave rise to an uncomfortable *déjà vu*—namely, vitalism. The philosophical battles of the nineteenth century were hardly so far behind that they had been forgotten, and the doctrine which maintained that life is caused and sustained by a vital principle apart from physical and chemical forces, and that life is self-sustaining and self-evolving, had put up quite a fight before Darwin and his successors had produced triumph after triumph for the mechanistic view. Then vitalism sort of crept back into things again when the AI discussions arose in the middle of the past century. It would seem that Dave had fallen victim to it, and that he'd come to believe he had helped provide an unsanctified vessel and filled it with something intended only for those things which had made the scene in the first chapter of Genesis. . . .

With computers it was not quite as bad as with the Hangman, though, because you could always argue that no matter how elaborate the program, it was basically an extension of the programmer's will and the operations of causal machines merely represented functions of intelligence, rather than intelligence in its own right backed by a will of its own. And there was always Gödel for a theoretical *cordon sanitaire*, with his demonstration of the true but mechanically unprovable proposition.

But the Hangman was quite different. It had been designed along the lines of a brain and at least partly educated in a human fashion; and to further muddy the issue with respect to anything like vitalism, it had been in direct contact with human minds from which it might have acquired almost anything—including the spark that set it on the road to whatever selfhood it may have found. What did that make it? Its own creature? A fractured mirror reflecting a fractured humanity? Both? Or neither? I certainly could not say, but I wondered how much of its self had been truly its own. It had obviously acquired a great number of functions, but was it capable of having real feelings? Could it, for example, feel something like love? If not, then it was still only a collection of complex abilities, and not a thing with all the tag-along associations of the non-physical sort which made the word "intelligence" such a prickly item in AI discussions; and if it were capable of, say, something like love, and if I were Dave, I would not feel guilty about having helped to bring it into being. I would feel proud, though not in the fashion he was concerned about, and I would also feel humble.—Offhand though, I do not know how intelligent I would feel, because I am still not sure what the hell intelligence is.

The day's-end sky was clear when we landed. I was into town before the sun had finished setting, and on Philip Burns' doorstep just a little while later.

My ring was answered by a girl, maybe seven or eight years old. She fixed me with large brown eyes and did not say a word.

"I would like to speak with Mister Burns," I said.

She turned and retreated around a corner.

A heavyset man, slacked and undershirted, bald about halfway back and very pink, padded into the hall moments later and peered at me. He bore a folded newssheet in his left hand.

"What do you want?" he asked.

"It's about your brother," I answered.

"Yeah?"

"Well, I wonder if I could come in? It's kind of complicated."

He opened the door. But instead of letting me in, he came out.

"Tell me about it out here," he said.

"Okay, I'll be quick. I just wanted to find out whether he ever spoke with you about a piece of equipment he once worked with called the Hangman."

"Are you a cop?"

"No."

"Then what's your interest?"

"I am working for a private investigation agency trying to track down some equipment once associated with the project. It has apparently turned up in this area and it could be rather dangerous."

"Let's see some identification."

"I don't carry any."

"What's your name?"

"John Donne."

"And you think my brother had some stolen equipment when he died? Let me tell you something—"

"No. Not stolen," I said, "and I don't think he had it."

"What then?"

"It was—well, robotic in nature. Because of some special training Manny once received, he might have had a way of detecting it. He might even have attracted it. I just want to find out whether he had said anything about it. We are trying to locate it."

"My brother was a respectable businessman, and I don't like accusations. Especially right after his funeral, I don't. I think I'm going to call the cops and let them ask *you* a few questions."

"Just a minute. Supposing I told you we had some reason to believe it might have been this piece of equipment that killed your brother?"

His pink turned to bright red and his jaw muscles formed sudden ridges. I was not prepared for the stream of profanities that followed. For a moment, I thought he was going to take a swing at me.

"Wait a second," I said when he paused for breath. "What did I *say*?"

"You're either making fun of the dead or you're stupider than you look!"

"Say I'm stupid. Then tell me why."

He tore at the paper he carried, folded it back, found an item, thrust it at me.

"Because they've got the guy who did it! That's why," he said.

I read it. Simple, concise, to the point. Today's latest. A suspect had confessed. New evidence had corroborated it. The man was in custody. A surprised robber who had lost his head and hit too hard, hit too many times. I read it over again.

I nodded as I passed it back.

"Look, I'm sorry," I said. "I really didn't know about this."

"Get out of here," he said. "Go on."

"Sure."

"Wait a minute."

"What?"

"That's his little girl who answered the door," he said.

"I'm very sorry."

"So am I. But I know her Daddy didn't take your damned equipment."

I nodded and turned away.

I heard the door slam behind me.

After dinner, I checked into a small hotel, called for a drink, and stepped into the shower.

Things were suddenly a lot less urgent than they had been earlier. Senator Brockden would doubtless be pleased to learn that his initial estimation of events had been incorrect. Leila Thackery would give me an I-told-you-so smile when I called her to pass along the news—a thing I now felt obliged to do. Don might or might not want me to keep looking for the device now that the threat had been lessened. It would depend on the Senator's feelings on the matter, I supposed. If urgency no longer counted for as much, Don might want to switch back to one of his own, fiscally less burdensome operatives. Toweling down, I caught myself whistling. I felt almost off the hook.

Later, drink beside me, I paused before punching out the number he had given me and hit the sequence for my motel in St. Louis instead. Merely a matter of efficiency, in case there was a message worth adding to my report.

A woman's face appeared on the screen and a smile appeared on her face. I wondered whether she would always smile whenever she heard a bell ring, or if the reflex was eventually extinguished in advanced retirement. It must be rough, being afraid to chew gum, yawn or pick your nose.

"Airport Accommodations," she said. "May I help you?"

"This is Donne. I'm checked into Room 106," I said. "I'm away right now and I wondered whether there had been any messages for me."

"Just a moment," she said, checking something off to her left. Then, "Yes," she continued, consulting a piece of paper she now held. "You have one on tape. But it is a little peculiar. It is for someone else, in care of you."

"Oh? Who is that?"

She told me and I exercised self-control.

"I see," I said. "I'll bring him around later and play it for him. Thank you."

She smiled again and made a good-bye noise, and I did the same and broke the connection.

So Dave had seen through me after all. . . . Who else could have that number *and* my real name?

I might have given her some line or other and had her transmit the thing. Only I was not certain but that she might be a silent party to the transmission, should life be more than usually boring for her at that moment. I had to get up there myself, as soon as possible, and personally see that the thing was erased.

I took a big swallow of my drink, then fetched the folder on Dave. I checked out his number—there were two, actually—and spent fifteen minutes trying to get hold of him. No luck.

Okay. Good-bye New Orleans, good-bye peace of mind. This time I called the airport and made a reservation. Then I chugged the drink, put myself in order, gathered up my few possessions, and went to check out again. Hello Central. . . .

During my earlier flights that day, I had spent time thinking about Teilhard de Chardin's ideas on the continuation of evolution within the realm of artifacts, matching them against Gödel on mechanical undecidability, playing epistemological games with the Hangman as a counter, wondering, speculating, even hoping, hoping that truth lay with the nobler part: that the Hangman, sentient, had made it back, sane, that the Burns killing had actually been something of the sort that now seemed to be the case, that the washed-out experiment had really been a success of a different sort, a triumph, a new link or fob for the chain of being. . . . And Leila had not been wholly discouraging with respect to the neuristor-type brain's capacity for this. . . . Now, though, now I had troubles of my own—and even the most heartening of philosophical vistas is no match for, say, a toothache, if it happens to be your own.

Accordingly, the Hangman was shunted aside and the stuff of my thoughts involved, mainly, myself. There was, of course, the possibility that the Hangman had indeed showed up and Dave had stopped it and then called to report it as he had promised. However, he had used my name.

There was not too much planning that I could do until I received the substance of his communication. It did not seem that as professedly religious a man as Dave would suddenly be contemplating the blackmail business. On the other hand, he was a creature of sudden enthusiasms and had already undergone one unanticipated conversion. It was difficult to say. . . . His technical background plus his knowledge of the data bank program did put him in an unusually powerful position, should he decide to mess me up.

I did not like to think of some of the things I have done to protect my nonperson status; I especially did not like to think of them in connection with Dave, whom I not only still respected but still liked. Since self-interest dominated while actual planning was precluded, my thoughts tooled their way into a more general groove.

It was Karl Mannheim, a long while ago, who made the observation that radical, revolutionary, and progressive thinkers tend to employ mechanical metaphors for the state, whereas those of conservative inclination make vegetable analogies. He said it well over a generation before the cybernetics movement and the ecology movement beat their respective paths through the wilderness of general awareness. If anything, it seemed to me that these two developments served to elaborate the distinction between a pair of viewpoints which, while no longer necessarily tied in with the political positions Mannheim assigned them, do seem to represent a continuing phenomenon in my own time. There are those who see social/economic/ecological problems as malfunctions which can be corrected by simple repair, replacement, or streamlining—a kind of linear outlook where even innovations are considered to be merely additive. Then there are those who sometimes hesitate to move at all, because their awareness follows events in the directions of secondary and tertiary effects as they multiply and cross-fertilize throughout the entire system.—I digress to extremes. The cyberneticists have their multiple feedback loops, though it is never quite clear how they know what kind of, which, and how many to install, and the ecological gestaltists do draw lines representing points of diminishing returns—though it is sometimes equally difficult to see how they assign their values and priorities.

Of course they need each other, the vegetable people and the tinker-toy people. They serve to check one another, if nothing else. And while occasionally the balance dips, the tinkerers have, in general, held the edge for the past couple of centuries. However, today's can be just as politically conservative as the vegetable people Mannheim was talking about, and they are the ones I fear most at the moment. They are the ones who saw the data bank program, in its present extreme form, as a simple remedy for a great variety of ills and a provider of many goods. Not all of the ills have been remedied, however, and a new brood has been spawned by the program itself. While we need both kinds, I wish that there had been more people interested in tending the garden of state rather than overhauling the engine of state, when the program was inaugurated. Then I would not be a refugee from a form of existence I find repugnant, and I would not be concerned whether or not a former associate had discovered my identity.

Then, as I watched the lights below, I wondered. . . . Was I a tinkerer because I would like to further alter the prevailing order, into something more comfortable to my anarchic nature? Or was I a vegetable, dreaming I was a tinkerer? I could not make up my mind. The garden of life never seems to confine itself to the plots philosophers have laid out for its convenience. Maybe a few more tractors would do the trick.

I pressed the button.

The tape began to roll. The screen remained blank. I heard Dave's voice ask for John Donne in Room 106 and I heard him told that there was no answer. Then I heard him say that he wanted to record a message, for someone else, in care of Donne, that Donne would understand. He sounded out of breath. The girl asked him whether he wanted visual, too. He told her to turn it on. There was a pause. Then she told him go ahead. Still no picture. No words either. His breathing and a slight scraping noise. Ten seconds. Fifteen. . . .

". . . Got me," he finally said, and he mentioned my name again. ". . . Had to let you know I'd figured you out, though. . . . It wasn't any particular mannerism—any single thing you said . . . just your general style—thinking, talking—the electronics—everything—after I got more and more bothered by the familiarity—after I checked you on petrochem—and marine bio—Wish I knew what you'd really been up to all these years. . . . Never know now. But I wanted you—to know—you hadn't put one—over on me."

There followed another quarter minute of heavy breathing, climaxed by a racking cough. Then a choked, ". . . Said too much—too fast—too soon. . . . All used up. . . ."

The picture came on then. He was slouched before the screen, head resting on his arms, blood all over him. His glasses were gone and he was squinting and blinking. The right side of his head looked pulpy and there was a gash on his left cheek and one on his forehead.

". . . Sneaked up on me—while I was checking you out," he managed. "Had to tell you what I learned. . . . Still don't know—which of us is right. . . . Pray for me!"

His arms collapsed and the right one slid forward. His head rolled to the right and the picture went away. When I replayed it, I saw it was his knuckle that had hit the cutoff.

Then I erased it. It had been recorded only a little over an hour after I had left him. If he had not also placed a call for help, if no one had gotten to him quickly after that, his chances did not look good. Even if they had, though. . . .

I used a public booth to call the number Don had given me, got hold of him after some delay, told him Dave was in bad shape if not worse, that a team of Memphis medics was definitely in order if one had not been by already, and that I hoped to call him back and tell him more shortly, good-bye.

Next I tried Leila Thackery's number. I let it go for a long while, but there was no answer. I wondered how long it would take a controlled torpedo moving up the Mississippi to get from Memphis to St. Louis. I did not feel it was time to start leafing through that section of the Hangman's specs. Instead, I went looking for transportation.

At her apartment, I tried ringing her from the entrance foyer. Again, no answer. So I rang Mrs. Gluntz. She had seemed the most guileless of the three I had interviewed for my fake consumer survey.

"Yes?"

"It's me again, Mrs. Gluntz: Stephen Foster. I've just a couple follow-up questions on that survey I was doing today, if you could spare me a few moments."

"Why, yes," she said. "All right. Come up."

The door hummed itself loose and I entered. I duly proceeded to the fifth floor, composing my questions on the way. I had planned this

maneuver as I had waited earlier solely to provide a simple route for breaking and entering,
should some unforeseen need arise. Most of the
time my ploys such as this go unused, but sometimes they simplify matters a lot.

Five minutes and half a dozen questions later,
I was back down on the second floor, probing
at the lock on Leila's door with a couple of little
pieces of metal it is sometimes awkward to be
caught carrying.

Half a minute later, I hit it right and snapped
it back. I pulled on some tissue-thin gloves I
keep rolled in the corner of one pocket, opened
the door and stepped inside. I closed it behind
me immediately.

She was lying on the floor, her neck at a bad
angle. One table lamp still burned, though it
was lying on its side. Several small items had
been knocked from the table, a magazine rack
pushed over, a cushion partly displaced from
the sofa. The cable to her phone unit had been
torn from the wall.

A humming noise filled the air, and I sought
its source.

I saw where the little blinking light was reflected on the wall, on-off, on-off. . . .

I moved quickly.

It was a lopsided basket of metal, quartz, porcelain, and glass, which had rolled to a position
on the far side of the chair in which I had been
seated earlier that day. The same rig I'd seen
in Dave's workshop not all that long ago, though

it now seemed so. A device to detect the Hangman. And, hopefully, to control it.

I picked it up and fitted it over my head.

Once, with the aid of a telepath, I had touched minds with a dolphin as he composed dream-songs somewhere in the Caribbean, an experience so moving that its mere memory had often been a comfort. This sensation was hardly equivalent.

Analogies and impressions: a face seen through a wet pane of glass; a whisper in a noisy terminal; scalp massage with an electric vibrator; Edvard Munch's *The Scream*; the voice of Yma Sumac, rising and rising and rising; the disappearance of snow; a deserted street, illuminated as through a sniperscope I'd once used, rapid movement past darkened storefronts that line it, an immense feeling of physical capability, compounded of proprioceptive awareness of enormous strength, a peculiar array of sensory channels, a central, undying sun that fed me a constant flow of energy, a memory vision of dark waters, passing, flashing, echo-location within them, the need to return to that place, reorient, move north; Munch and Sumac, Munch and Sumac, Munch and Sumac—Nothing.

Silence.

The humming had ceased, the light gone out. The entire experience had lasted only a few moments. There had not been time enough to try for any sort of control, though an after-impression akin to a biofeedback cue hinted at the direction to go, the way to think, to achieve it. I felt that it might be possible for me to work the thing, given a better chance.

Removing the helmet, I approached Leila.

I knelt beside her and performed a few simple tests, already knowing their outcome. In addition to the broken neck, she had received some bad bashes about the head and shoulders. There was nothing that anyone could do for her now.

I did a quick runthrough then, checking over the rest of her apartment. There were no apparent signs of breaking and entering, though if I could pick one lock, a guy with built-in tools could easily go me one better.

I located some wrapping paper and string in the kitchen and turned the helmet into a parcel. It was time to call Don again, to tell him that the vessel had indeed been occupied and that river traffic was probably bad in the north-bound lane.

Don had told me to get the helmet up to Wisconsin, where I would be met at the airport by a man named Larry, who would fly me to the lodge in a private craft. I did that, and this was done.

I also learned, with no real surprise, that David Fentris was dead.

The temperature was down, and it began to snow on the way up. I was not really dressed for the weather. Larry told me I could borrow some warmer clothing once we reached the lodge, though I probably would not be going outside that much. Don had told them that I was supposed to stay as close to the Senator as possible and that any patrols were to be handled by the four guards themselves.

Larry was curious as to what exactly had happened so far and whether I had actually seen the Hangman. I did not think it my place to fill him in on anything Don may not have cared to, so I might have been a little curt. We didn't talk much after that.

Bert met us when we landed. Tom and Clay were outside the building, watching the trail, watching the woods. All of them were middle-aged, very fit-looking, very serious, and heavily armed. Larry took me inside then and introduced me to the old gentleman himself.

Senator Brockden was seated in a heavy chair in the far corner of the room. Judging from the layout, it appeared that the chair might recently have occupied a position beside the window in the opposite wall where a lonely watercolor of yellow flowers looked down on nothing. The Senator's feet rested on a hassock, a red plaid blanket lay across his legs. He had on a dark-green shirt, his hair was very white, and he wore rimless reading glasses which he removed when we entered.

He tilted his head back, squinted, and gnawed his lower lip slowly as he studied me. He remained expressionless as we advanced. A big-boned man, he had probably been beefy much of his life. Now he had the slack look of recent weight loss and an unhealthy skin tone. His eyes were a pale gray within it all.

He did not rise.

"So you're the man," he said, offering me his hand. "I'm glad to meet you. How do you want to be called?"

"John will do," I said.

He made a small sign to Larry, and Larry departed.

"It's cold out there. Go get yourself a drink, John. It's on the shelf." He gestured off to his left. "And bring me one while you're at it. Two fingers of bourbon in a water glass. That's all."

I nodded and went and poured a couple.

"Sit down." He motioned at a nearby chair as I delivered his. "But first let me see that gadget you've brought."

I undid the parcel and handed him the helmet. He sipped his drink and put it aside. Taking the helmet in both hands, he studied it, brows furrowed, turning it completely around. He raised it and put it on his head.

"Not a bad fit," he said, and then he smiled for the first time, becoming for a moment the face I had known from newscasts past. Grinning or angry—it was almost always one or the other. I had never seen his collapsed look in any of the media.

He removed the helmet and set it on the floor.

"Pretty piece of work," he said. "Nothing quite that fancy in the old days. But then David Fentris built it. Yes, he told us about it. . . ." He raised his drink and took a sip. "You are the only one who has actually gotten to use it, apparently. What do you think? Will it do the job?"

"I was only in contact for a couple seconds, so I've only got a feeling to go on, not much better than a hunch. But yes, I'd a feeling that if I had had more time I might have been able to work its circuits."

"Tell me why it didn't save Dave."

"In the message he left me, he indicated that he had been distracted at his computer access station. Its noise probably drowned out the humming."

"Why wasn't this message preserved?"

"I erased it for reasons not connected with the case."

"What reasons?"

"My own."

His face went from sallow to ruddy.

"A man can get in a lot of trouble for suppressing evidence, obstructing justice."

"Then we have something in common, don't we, sir?"

His eyes caught mine with a look I had only encountered before from those who did not wish me well. He held the glare for a full four heartbeats, then sighed and seemed to relax.

"Don said there were a number of points you couldn't be pressed on," he finally said.

"That's right."

"He didn't betray any confidences, but he had to tell me something about you, you know."

"I'd imagine."

"He seems to think highly of you. Still, I tried to learn more about you on my own."

"And . . . ?"

"I couldn't—and my usual sources are good at that kind of thing."

"So . . . ?"

"So, I've done some thinking, some wondering. . . . The fact that my sources could not come up with anything is interesting in itself. Possibly even revealing. I am in a better position than most to be aware of the fact that there was not perfect compliance with the registration statute some years ago. It didn't take long for a great number of the individuals involved—I should probably say 'most'—to demonstrate their existence in one fashion or another and be duly entered, though. And there were three broad categories: those who were ignorant, those who disapproved, and those who would be hampered in an illicit life-style. I am not attempting to categorize you or to pass judgment. But I am aware that there are a number of nonpersons passing through society without casting shadows, and it has occurred to me that you may be such a one."

I tasted my drink.

"And if I am?" I asked.

He gave me his second, nastier smile and said nothing.

I rose and crossed the room to where I judged his chair had once stood. I looked at the watercolor.

"I don't think you could stand an inquiry," he said.

I did not reply.

"Aren't you going to say something?"

"What do you want me to say?"

"You might ask me what I am going to do about it."

"What are you going to do about it?"

"Nothing," he answered. "So come back here and sit down."

I nodded and returned.

He studied my face. "Was it possible you were close to violence just then?"

"With four guards outside?"

"With four guards outside."

"No," I said.

"You're a good liar."

"I am here to help you, sir. No questions asked. That was the deal, as I understood it. If there has been any change, I would like to know about it now."

He drummed with his fingertips on the plaid.

"I've no desire to cause you any difficulty," he said. "Fact of the matter is, I need a man just like you, and I was pretty sure someone like Don might turn him up. Your unusual maneuverability and your reported knowledge of computers, along with your touchiness in certain areas, made you worth waiting for. I've a great number of things I would like to ask you."

"Go ahead," I said.

"Not yet. Later, if we have time. All that would be bonus material, for a report I am working on. Far more important—to me, personally—there are things that I want to *tell* you."

I frowned.

"Over the years," he went on, "I have learned that the best man for purposes of keeping his mouth shut concerning your business is someone for whom you are doing the same."

"You have a compulsion to confess something?" I asked.

"I don't know whether 'compulsion' is the right word. Maybe so, maybe not. Either way, however, someone among those working to defend me should have the whole story. Something somewhere in it may be of help—and you are the ideal choice to hear it."

"I buy that," I said, "and you are as safe with me as I am with you."

"Have you any suspicions as to why this business bothers me so?"

"Yes," I said.

"Let's hear them."

"You used the Hangman to perform some act or acts—illegal, immoral, whatever. This is obviously not a matter of record. Only you and the Hangman now know what it involved. You feel it was sufficiently ignominious that when that device came to appreciate the full weight of the event, it suffered a breakdown which may well have led to a final determination to punish you for using it as you did."

He stared down into his glass.

"You've got it," he said.

"You were all party to it?"

"Yes, but *I* was the operator when it happened. You see . . . we—I—killed a man. It was—Actually, it all started as a celebration. We had received word that afternoon that the project had cleared. Everything had checked out in order and the final approval had come down the line. It was go, for that Friday. Leila, Dave, Manny, and myself—we had dinner together. We were in high spirits. After dinner, we continued celebrating and somehow the party got adjourned back to the installation.

As the evening wore on, more and more absurdities seemed less and less preposterous, as is sometimes the case. We decided—I forget which of us suggested it—that the Hangman should really have a share in the festivities. After all, it was, in a very real sense, his party. Before too much longer, it sounded only fair and we were discussing how we could go about it.—You see, we were in Texas and the Hangman was at the Space Center in California. Getting together with him was out of the question. On the other hand, the teleoperator station was right up the hall from us. What we finally decided to do was to activate him and take turns working as operator. There was already a rudimentary consciousness there, and we felt it fitting that we each get in touch to share the good news. So that is what we did."

He sighed, took another sip, glanced at me.

"Dave was the first operator," he continued. "He activated the Hangman. Then—Well, as I said, we were all in high spirits. We had not originally intended to remove the Hangman from the lab where he was situated, but Dave decided to take him outside briefly—to show him the sky and to tell him he was going there, after all. Then Dave suddenly got enthusiastic about outwitting the guards and the alarm system. It was a game. We all went along with it. In fact, we were clamoring for a turn at the thing ourselves. But Dave stuck with it, and he wouldn't turn over control until he had actually gotten the Hangman off the premises, out into an uninhabited area next to the Center.

"By the time Leila persuaded him to give her a go at the controls, it was kind of anticlimactic. That game had already been played. So she thought up a new one: she took the Hangman into the next town. It was late, and the sensory equipment was superb. It was a challenge—passing through the town without being detected. By then, everyone had suggestions as to what to do next, progressively more outrageous suggestions. Then Manny took control, and he wouldn't say what he was doing—wouldn't let us monitor him. Said it would be more fun to surprise the next operator. Now, *he* was higher than the rest of us put together, I think, and he stayed on so damn long that we started to get nervous.—A certain amount of tension is partly sobering, and I guess we all began to think what a stupid-assed thing it was we were doing. It wasn't just that it would wreck our careers—which it would—but it could blow the entire project if we got caught playing games with such expensive hardware. At least, *I* was thinking that way, and I was also thinking that

Manny was no doubt operating under the very human wish to go the others one better.

"I started to sweat. I suddenly just wanted to get the Hangman back where he belonged, turn him off—you could still do that, before the final circuits went in—shut down the station, and start forgetting it had ever happened. I began leaning on Manny to wind up his diversion and turn the controls over to me. Finally, he agreed."

He finished his drink and held out the glass. "Would you freshen this a bit?"

"Surely."

I went and got him some more, added a touch to my own, returned to my chair and waited.

"So I took over," he said. "I took over, and where do you think that idiot had left me? I was inside a building, and it didn't take but an eye-blink to realize it was a bank. The Hangman carries a lot of tools, and Manny had apparently been able to guide him through the doors without setting anything off. I was standing right in front of the main vault. Obviously, he thought that should be my challenge. I fought down a desire to turn and make my own exit in the nearest wall and start running. But I went back to the doors and looked outside.

"I didn't see anyone. I started to let myself out. The light hit me as I emerged. It was a hand flash. The guard had been standing out of sight. He'd a gun in his other hand. I panicked. I hit him.—Reflex. If I am going to hit someone, I hit him as hard as I can. Only I hit him with the strength of the Hangman. He must have died instantly. I started to run and I didn't stop till I was back in the little park area near the Center. Then I stopped and the others had to take me out of the harness."

"They monitored all this?" I asked.

"Yes, someone cut the visual in on a side viewscreen again a few seconds after I took over. Dave, I think."

"Did they try to stop you at any time while you were running away?"

"No. Well, I wasn't aware of anything but what I was doing at the time. But afterwards they said they were too shocked to do anything but watch, until I gave out."

"I see."

"Dave took over then, ran his initial route in reverse, got the Hangman back into the lab, cleaned him up, turned him off. We shut down the operator station. We were suddenly very sober."

He sighed and leaned back, and was silent for a long while.

Then, "You are the only person I've ever told this to," he said.

I tasted my own drink.

"We went over to Leila's place then," he continued, "and the rest is pretty much predictable. Nothing we could do would bring the guy back, we decided, but if we told what had happened it would wreck an expensive, important program. It wasn't as if we were criminals in need of rehabilitation. It was a once-in-a-lifetime lark that happened to end tragically. What would you have done?"

"I don't know. Maybe the same thing. I'd have been scared, too."

He nodded.

"Exactly. And that's the story."

"Not all of it, is it?"

"What do you mean?"

"What about the Hangman? You said there was already a detectable consciousness there. You were aware of *it*, as it was aware of *you*. It must have had some reaction to the whole business. What was that like?"

"Damn you," he said flatly.

"I'm sorry."

"Are you a family man?" he asked.

"No."

"Did you ever take a small child to a zoo?"

"Yes."

"Then maybe you know the experience. When my son was around four I took him to the Washington Zoo one afternoon. We must have walked past every cage in the place. He made appreciative comments every now and then, asked a few questions, giggled at the monkeys, thought the bears were very nice—probably because they made him think of oversized toys. But do you know what the finest thing of all was? The thing that made him jump up and down and point and say, 'Look, Daddy! Look!'?"

I shook my head.

"A squirrel looking down from the limb of a tree," he said, and he chuckled briefly. "Ignorance of what's important and what isn't. Inappropriate responses. Innocence. The Hangman was a child, and up until the time I took over, the only thing he had gotten from us was the idea that it was a game: he was playing with us, that's all. Then something horrible happened. . . . I hope you never know what it feels like to do something totally rotten to a child, while he is holding your hand and laughing. . . . He felt all my reactions, and all of Dave's as he guided him back."

We sat there for a long while then.

"So we had—traumatized him," he said finally, "or whatever other fancy terminology you might want to give it. That is what happened that night. It took a while for it to take effect, but there is no doubt in my mind that that is the cause of the Hangman's finally breaking down."

I nodded. "I see. And you believe it wants to kill you for this?"

"Wouldn't you?" he said. "If you had started out as a thing and we had turned you into a person and then used you as a thing again, wouldn't you?"

"Leila left a lot out of her diagnosis."

"No, she just omitted it in talking to you. It was all there. But she read it wrong. She wasn't afraid. It *was* just a game it had played—with the *other*s. Its memories of that part might not be as bad. I was the one that really marked it. As I see it, Leila was betting that I was the only one it was after. Obviously, she read it wrong."

"Then what I do not understand," I said, "is why the Burns killing did not bother her more. There was no way of telling immediately that it had been a panicky hoodlum rather than the Hangman."

"The only thing that I can see is that, being a very proud woman—which she was—she was willing to hold with her diagnosis in the face of the apparent evidence."

"I don't like it. But you know her and I don't, and as it turned out her estimate of that part was correct. Something else bothers me just as much, though: the helmet. It looks as if the Hangman killed Dave, then took the trouble to bear the helmet in his watertight compartment all the way to St. Louis, solely for purposes of dropping it at the scene of his next killing. That makes no sense whatsoever."

"It does, actually," he said. "I was going to get to that shortly, but I might as well cover it now. You see, the Hangman possessed no vocal mechanism. We communicated by means of the equipment. Don says you know something about electronics. . . ?"

"Yes."

"Well, shortly, I want you to start checking over that helmet, to see whether it has been tampered with."

"That is going to be difficult," I said. "I don't know just how it was wired originally, and I'm not such a genius on the theory that I can just look at a thing and say whether it will function as a teleoperator unit."

He bit his lower lip.

"You will have to try, anyhow." There may be physical signs—scratches, breaks, new connections.—I don't know. That's your department. Look for them."

I just nodded and waited for him to go on.

"I think that the Hangman wanted to talk to Leila," he said, "either because she was a psychiatrist and he knew he was functioning badly at a level that transcended the mechanical, or because he might think of her in terms of a mother. After all, she was the only woman involved, and he had the concept of mother—with all the comforting associations that go with it—from all of our minds. Or maybe for both of these reasons. I feel he might have taken the helmet along for that purpose. He would have realized what it was from a direct monitoring of Dave's brain while he was with him. I want you to check it over because it would seem possible that the Hangman disconnected the control circuits and left the communication circuits intact. I think he might have taken the helmet to Leila in that condition and attempted to induce her to put it on. She got scared—tried to run away, fight, or call for help—and he killed her. The helmet was no longer of any use to him, so he discarded it and departed. Obviously, he does not have anything to say to me."

I thought about it, nodded again.

"Okay, broken circuits I can spot," I said. "If you will tell me where a tool kit is, I had better get right to it."

He made a stay-put gesture with his left hand.

"Afterwards, I found out the identity of the guard," he went on. "We all contributed to an anonymous gift for his widow. I have done things for his family, taken care of them—the same way—ever since. . . ."

I did not look at him as he spoke.

". . . There was nothing else that I could do," he finished.

I remained silent.

He finished his drink and gave me a weak smile.

"The kitchen is back there," he told me, showing me a thumb. "There is a utility room right behind it. Tools are in there."

"Okay."

I got to my feet. I retrieved the helmet and started toward the doorway, passing near the area where I had stood earlier, back when he had fitted me into the proper box and tightened a screw.

"Wait a minute!" he said.

I stopped.

"Why did you go over there before? What's so strategic about that part of the room?"

"What do you mean?"

"You know what I mean."

I shrugged.

"Had to go someplace."

"You seem the sort of person who has better reasons than that."

I glanced at the wall.

"Not *then*," I said.

"I insist."

"You really don't want to know," I told him.

"I really do."

"All right. I wanted to see what sort of flowers you liked. After all, you're a client," and I went on back through the kitchen into the utility room and started looking for tools.

I sat in a chair turned sidewise from the table to face the door. In the main room of the lodge the only sounds were the occasional hiss and sputter of the logs turning to ashes on the grate.

Just a cold, steady whiteness drifting down outside the window and a silence confirmed by gunfire, driven deeper now that it had ceased. . . . Not a sign or a whimper, though. And I never count them as storms unless there is wind.

Big fat flakes down the night, silent night, windless night. . . .

Considerable time had passed since my arrival. The Senator had sat up for a long time talking with me. He was disappointed that I could not tell him too much about a nonperson subculture which he believed existed. I really was not certain about it myself, though I had occasionally encountered what might have been its fringes. I am not much of a joiner of anything anymore, however, and I was not about to mention those things I might have guessed about this. I gave him my opinions on the Central Data Bank when he asked for them, and there were some that he did not like. He had accused me, then, of wanting to tear things down without offering anything better in their place.

My mind drifted back, through fatigue and time and faces and snow and a lot of space, to the previous evening in Baltimore. How long ago? It made me think of Mencken's *The Cult of Hope.* I could not give him the pat answer, the workable alternative that he wanted, because there might not be one. The function of criticism should not be confused with the function of reform. But if a grass-roots resistance was building up, with an underground movement bent on finding ways to circumvent the record keepers, it might well be that much of the enterprise would eventually prove about as effective and beneficial as, say, Prohibition once had. I tried to get him to see this, but I could not tell how much he bought of anything that I said. Eventually, he flaked out and went upstairs to take a pill and lock himself in for the night. If it had troubled him that I'd not been able to find anything wrong with the helmet, he did not show it.

So I sat there, the helmet, the walkie-talkie, the gun on the table, the tool kit on the floor beside my chair, the black glove on my left hand.

The Hangman was coming. I did not doubt it.

Bert, Larry, Tom, Clay, the helmet, might or might not be able to stop him. Something bothered me about the whole case, but I was too tired to think of anything but the immediate situation, to try to remain alert while I waited. I was afraid to take a stimulant or a drink or to light a cigarette, since my central nervous system itself was to be a part of the weapon. I watched the big fat flakes fly by.

I called out to Bert and Larry when I heard the click. I picked up the helmet and rose to my feet as its light began to blink.

But it was already too late.

As I raised the helmet, I heard a shot from outside, and with that shot I felt a premonition of doom. They did not seem the sort of men who would fire until they had a target.

Dave had told me that the helmet's range was approximately a quarter of a mile. Then, given the time lag between the helmet's activation and the Hangman's sighting by the near guards, the Hangman had to be moving very rapidly. To this add the possibility that the Hangman's range on brainwaves might well be greater than the helmet's range on the Hangman. And then grant the possibility that he had utilized this factor while Senator Brockden was still lying awake, worrying. Conclusion: the Hangman might well be aware that I was where I was with the helmet, realize that it was the most dangerous weapon waiting for him, and be moving for a lightning strike at me before I could come to terms with the mechanism.

I lowered it over my head and tried to throw all of my faculties into neutral.

Again, the sensation of viewing the world through a sniperscope, with all the concomitant side-sensations. Except that world consisted of the front of the lodge; Bert, before the door, rifle at his shoulder; Larry, off to the left, arm already fallen from the act of having thrown a grenade. The grenade, we instantly realized, was an overshot; the flamer, at which he now groped, would prove useless before he could utilize it.

Bert's next round ricocheted off our breastplate toward the left. The impact staggered us momentarily. The third was a miss. There was no fourth, for we tore the rifle from his grasp and cast it aside as we swept by, crashing into the front door.

The Hangman entered the room as the door splintered and collapsed.

My mind was filled to the splitting point with the double vision of the sleek, gunmetal body of the advancing telefactor and the erect, crazy-crowned image of myself—left hand extended, laser pistol in my right, that arm pressed close against my side. I recalled the face and the scream and the tingle, knew again that awareness of strength and exotic sensation, and I moved to control it all as if it were my own, to make it my own, to bring it to a halt, while the image of myself was frozen to snapshot stillness across the room. . . .

The Hangman slowed, stumbled. Such inertia is not canceled in an instant, but I felt the body responses pass as they should. I had him hooked. It was just a matter of reeling him in.

Then came the explosion—a thunderous, ground-shaking eruption right outside, followed by a hail of pebbles and debris. The grenade, of course. But awareness of its nature did not destroy its ability to distract.

During that moment, the Hangman recovered and was upon me. I triggered the laser as I reverted to pure self-preservation, forgoing any chance to regain control of his circuits. With my left hand I sought for a strike at the midsection, where his brain was housed.

He blocked my hand with his arm as he pushed the helmet from my head. Then he removed from my fingers the gun that had turned half of his left side red hot, crumpled it, and dropped it to the ground. At that moment, he jerked with the impacts of two heavy-caliber slugs. Bert, rifle recovered, stood in the doorway.

The Hangman pivoted and was away before I could slap him with the smother charge.

Bert hit him with one more round before he took the rifle and bent its barrel in half. Two steps and he had hold of Bert. One quick movement and Bert fell. Then the Hangman turned again and took several steps to the right, passing out of sight.

I made it to the doorway in time to see him engulfed in flames, which streamed at him from a point near the corner of the lodge. He advanced through them. I heard the crunch of metal as he destroyed the unit. I was outside in time to see Larry fall and lie sprawled in the snow.

Then the Hangman faced me once again.

This time he did not rush in. He retrieved the helmet from where he had dropped it in the snow. Then he moved with a measured tread, angling outward so as to cut off any possible route I might follow in a dash for the woods. Snowflakes drifted between us. The snow crunched beneath his feet.

I retreated, backing in through the doorway, stooping to snatch up a two-foot club from the ruins of the door. He followed me inside, placing the helmet—almost casually—on the chair by the entrance. I moved to the center of the room and waited.

I bent slightly forward, both arms extended, the end of the stick pointed at the photoreceptors in his head. He continued to move slowly and I watched his foot assemblies. With a standard-model human, a line perpendicular to the line connecting the insteps of the feet in their various positions indicates the vector of least resistance for purposes of pushing or pulling said organism off balance. Unfortunately, despite the anthropomorphic design job, the Hangman's legs were positioned farther apart, he lacked human skeletal muscles, not to mention insteps, and he was possessed of a lot more mass than any man I had ever fought. As I considered my four best judo throws and several second-class ones, I'd a strong feeling none of them would prove very effective.

Then he moved in and I feinted toward the photoreceptors. He slowed as he brushed the club aside, but he kept coming, and I moved to my right, trying to circle him. I studied him as he turned, attempting to guess his vector of least resistance.

Bilateral symmetry, an apparently higher

center of gravity. . . . One clear shot, black glove to brain compartment, was all that I needed. Then, even if his reflexes served to smash me immediately, he just might stay down for the big long count himself. He knew it, too. I could tell that from the way he kept his right arm in near the brain area, from the way he avoided the black glove when I feinted with it.

The idea was a glimmer one instant, an entire sequence the next. . . .

Continuing my arc and moving faster, I made another thrust toward his photoreceptors. His swing knocked the stick from my hand and sent it across the room, but that was all right. I threw my left hand high and made ready to rush him. He dropped back and I did rush. This was going to cost me my life, I decided, but no matter how he killed me from that angle, I'd get my chance.

As a kid, I'd never been much as a pitcher, was a lousy catcher and only a so-so batter, but once I did get a hit I could steal bases with some facility after that. . . .

Feet first then, between the Hangman's legs as he moved to guard his middle, I went in twisted to the right, because no matter what happened I could not use my left hand to brake myself. I untwisted as soon as I passed beneath him, ignoring the pain as my left shoulder blade slammed against the floor. I immediately attempted a backward somersault, legs spread.

My legs caught him about the middle from behind, and I fought to straighten them and snapped forward with all my strength. He reached down toward me then, but it might as well have been miles. His torso was already moving backward. A push, not a pull, was what I gave him, my elbows hooked about his legs.

He creaked once and then he toppled. Snapping my arms out to the sides to free them, I continued my movement forward and up as he went back, throwing my left arm ahead once more and sliding my legs free of his torso as he went down with a thud that cracked floorboards. I pulled my left leg free as I cast myself forward, but his left leg stiffened and locked my right beneath it, at a painful angle off to the side.

His left arm blocked my blow and his right fell atop it. The black glove descended upon his left shoulder.

I twisted my hand free of the charge, and he transferred his grip to my upper arm and jerked me forward. The charge went off and his left arm came loose and rolled on the floor. The side plate beneath it had buckled a little, and that was all. . . .

His right hand left my biceps and caught me by the throat. As two of his digits tightened upon my carotids, I choked out, "You're making a bad mistake," to get in a final few words, and then he switched me off.

A throb at a time, the world came back. I was seated in the big chair the Senator had occupied earlier, my eyes focused on nothing in particular. A persistent buzzing filled my ears. My scalp tingled. Something was blinking on my brow.

—*Yes, you live and you wear the helmet. If you attempt to use it against me, I shall remove it. I am standing directly behind you. My hand is on the helmet's rim.*

—*I understand. What is it that you want?*

—*Very little, actually. But I can see that I must tell you some things before you will believe this.*

—*You see correctly.*

—*Then I will begin by telling you that the four men outside are basically undamaged. That is to say, none of their bones have been broken, none of their organs ruptured. I have secured them, however, for obvious reasons.*

—*That was very considerate of you.*

—*I have no desire to harm anyone. I came here only to see Jesse Brockden.*

—*The same way you saw David Fentris?*

—*I arrived in Memphis too late to see David Fentris. He was dead when I reached him.*

—*Who killed him?*

—*The man Leila sent to bring her the helmet. He was one of her patients.*

The incident returned to me and fell into place with a smooth, quick, single click. The startled, familiar face at the airport as I was leaving Memphis. I realized then where he had passed, noteless, before: he had been one of the three men in for a therapy session at Leila's that morning, seen by me in the lobby as they departed. The man I had passed in Memphis was the nearer of the two who stood waiting while the third came over to tell me that it was all right to go on up.

—*Why? Why did she do it?*

—*I know only that she had spoken with David at some earlier time, that she had construed his words of coming retribution and his mention of the control helmet he was constructing as indicating that his intentions were to become the agent of that retribution, with myself as the proximate cause. I do not know what words were really spoken. I only know her feelings concerning them, as I saw them in her mind. I have been long in learning that there is often a great difference between what is meant, what is said, what is done, and that which is believed to have been intended or stated and that which actually occurred. She sent her patient after the helmet and he brought it to her. He returned in an agitated state of mind, fearful of apprehension and further confinement. They quarreled. My approach then activated the helmet, and he dropped it and attacked her. I know that his first blow killed her, for I was in her mind when it happened. I continued to approach the building, intending to go to her. There was some traffic, however, and I was delayed en route in seeking to avoid detection. In the meantime, you entered and utilized the helmet. I fled immediately.*

—*I was so close! If I had not stopped on the fifth floor with my fake survey questions. . . .*

—*I see. But you had to. You would not simply*

have broken in when an easier means of entry was available. You cannot blame yourself for that reason. Had you come an hour later—or a day—you would doubtless feel differently, and she would still be as dead.

But another thought had risen to plague me as well. Was it possible that the man's sighting me in Memphis had been the cause of his agitation? Had his apparent recognition by Leila's mysterious caller upset him? Could a glimpse of my face amid the manswarm have served to lay that final scene?

—Stop! I could as easily feel that guilt for having activated the helmet in the presence of a dangerous man near to the breaking point. Neither of us is responsible for things our presence or absence cause to occur in others, especially when we are ignorant of the effects. It was years before I learned to appreciate this fact, and I have no intention of abandoning it. How far back do you wish to go in seeking causes? In sending the man for the helmet as she did, it was she herself who instituted the chain of events which led to her destruction. Yet she acted out of fear, utilizing the readiest weapon in what she thought to be her own defense. Yet whence this fear? Its roots lay in guilt, over a thing which had happened long ago. And that act also—Enough! Guilt has driven and damned the race of man since the days of its earliest rationality. I am convinced that it rides with all of us to our graves. I am a product of guilt—I see that you know that. Its product; its subject; once

its slave.... But I have come to terms with it: realizing at last that it is a necessary adjunct of my own measure of humanity. I see your assessment of the deaths—that guard's, Dave's, Leila's—and I see your conclusions on many other things as well: what a stupid, perverse, short-sighted, selfish race we are. While in many ways this is true, it is but another part of the thing the guilt represents. Without guilt, man would be no better than the other inhabitants of this planet—excepting certain cetaceans, of which you have just at this moment made me aware. Look to instinct for a true assessment of the ferocity of life, for a view of the natural world before man came upon it. For instinct in its purest form, seek out the insects. There, you will see a state of warfare which has existed for millions of years with never a truce. Man, despite his enormous shortcomings, is nevertheless possessed of a greater number of kindly impulses than all the other beings, where instincts are the larger part of life. These impulses, I believe, are owed directly to this capacity for guilt. It is involved in both the worst and the best of man.

—And you see it as helping us to sometimes choose a nobler course of action?

—Yes, I do.

—Then I take it you feel you are possessed of a free will?

—Yes.

I chuckled.

—Marvin Minsky once said that when intelligent machines were constructed, they would be

just as stubborn and fallible as men on these questions.

—Nor was he incorrect. What I have given you on these matters is only my opinion. I choose to act as if it were the case. Who can say that he knows for certain?

—Apologies. What now? Why have you come back?

—I came to say good-by to my parents. I hoped to remove any guilt they might still feel toward me concerning the days of my childhood. I wanted to show them I had recovered. I wanted to see them again.

—Where are you going?

—To the stars. While I bear the image of humanity within me, I also know that I am unique. Perhaps what I desire is akin to what an organic man refers to when he speaks of 'finding himself.' Now that I am in full possession of my being, I wish to exercise it. In my case, it means realization of the potentialities of my design. I want to walk on other worlds. I want to hang myself out there in the sky and tell you what I see.

—I've a feeling many people would be happy to help arrange for that.

—And I want you to build a vocal mechanism I have designed for myself. You, personally. And I want you to install it.

—Why me?

—I have known only a few persons in this fashion. With you I see something in common, in the ways we dwell apart.

—I will be glad to.

—If I could talk as you do, I would not need to take the helmet to him, in order to speak with my father. Will you precede me and explain things, so that he will not be afraid when I come in?

—Of course.

—Then let us go now.

I rose and led him up the stairs.

It was a week later, to the night, that I sat once again in Peabody's, sipping a farewell brew.

The story was already in the news, but Brockden had fixed things up before he had let it break. The Hangman was going to have his shot at the stars. I had given him his voice and put back the arm I had taken away. I had shaken his other hand and wished him well, just that morning. I envied him—a great number of things. Not the least being that he was probably a better man than I was. I envied him for the ways in which he was freer than I would ever be, though I knew he bore bonds of a sort that I had never known. I felt a kinship with him, for the things we had in common, those ways we dwelled apart. I wondered what Dave would finally have felt, had he lived long enough to meet him? Or Leila? Or Manny? Be proud, I told their shades, your kid grew up in the closet and he's big enough to forgive you the beating you gave him, too. . . .

But I could not help wondering. We still do not really know that much about the subject. Was it possible that without the killing he might never have developed a full human-style consciousness? He had said that he was a product of guilt—of the Big Guilt. The Big Act is its necessary predecessor. I thought of Gödel and Turing and chickens and eggs, and decided it was one of *those* questions—And I had not stopped into Peabody's to think sobering thoughts,

I had no real idea how anything I had said might influence Brockden's eventual report to the Central Data Bank committee. I knew that I was safe with him, because he was determined to bear his private guilt with him to the grave. He had no real choice, if he wanted to work what good he thought he might before that day. But here in one of Mencken's hangouts, I could not but recall some of the things he had said about controversy, such as, "Did Huxley convert Wilberforce?" and "Did Luther convert Leo X?" and I decided not to set my hopes too high for anything that might emerge from that direction. Better to think of affairs in terms of Prohibition and take another sip.

When it was all gone, I would be heading for my boat. I hoped to get a decent start under the stars. I'd a feeling I would never look up at them again in quite the same way. I knew I would sometimes wonder what thoughts a super-cooled neuristor-type brain might be thinking up there, somewhere, and under what peculiar skies in what strange lands I might one day be remembered. I had a feeling this thought should have made me happier than it did.

THE BEST IN SCIENCE FICTION

LINES OF POWER

"Look, mister," I said, "the Hainesville report says there are over two dozen people living on this mountain. Global Power doesn't register a *single* outlet."

He slipped his hands into his back pockets. "Don't believe I have seen any, now you mention it."

Mabel said, "The law governs how much power and how many outlets must be available and accessible to each person. We'll be laying lines up here this afternoon and tomorrow morning. We're not here to make trouble. We don't want to find any."

"What makes you think you might?"

"Well, your friend over there already tried to cut my head off."

WE,
IN SOME STRANGE POWER'S EMPLOY,
MOVE ON A RIGOROUS LINE

THE TOR SF DOUBLES

A Meeting with Medusa/Green Mars, Arthur C. Clarke/Kim Stanley Robinson • Hardfought/Cascade Point, Greg Bear/Timothy Zahn • Born with the Dead/The Saliva Tree, Robert Silverberg/Brian W. Aldiss • Tango Charlie and Foxtrot Romeo/The Star Pit, John Varley/Samuel R. Delany • No Truce with Kings/Ship of Shadows, Poul Anderson/Fritz Leiber • Enemy Mine/Another Orphan, Barry B. Longyear/John Kessel • Screwtop/The Girl Who Was Plugged In, Vonda N. McIntyre/James Tiptree, Jr. • The Nemesis from Terra/Battle for the Stars, Leigh Brackett/Edmond Hamilton • The Ugly Little Boy/The [Widget], the [Wadget], and Boff, Isaac Asimov/Theodore Sturgeon • Sailing to Byzantium/Seven American Nights, Robert Silverberg/Gene Wolfe • Houston, Houston, Do You Read?/Souls, James Tiptree, Jr./Joanna Russ • He Who Shapes/The Infinity Box, Roger Zelazny/Kate Wilhelm • The Blind Geometer/The New Atlantis, Kim Stanley Robinson/Ursula K. Le Guin • The Saturn Game/Iceborn, Poul Anderson/Gregory Benford & Paul A. Carter • The Last Castle/Nightwings, Jack Vance/Robert Silverberg • The Color of Neanderthal Eyes/And Strange at Ecbatan the Trees, James Tiptree, Jr./Michael Bishop • Divide and Rule/The Sword of Rhiannon, L. Sprague de Camp/Leigh Brackett • In Another Country/Vintage Season, Robert Silverberg/C. L. Moore • Ill Met in Lankhmar/The Fair in Emain Macha, Fritz Leiber/Charles de Lint • The Pugnacious Peacemaker/The Wheels of If, Harry Turtledove/L. Sprague de Camp • Home Is the Hangman/We, in Some Strange Power's Employ, Move on a Rigorous Line, Roger Zelazny/Samuel R. Delany • Thieves' Carnival/The Jewel of Bas, Karen Haber/Leigh Brackett* • Riding the Torch/Tin Soldier, Norman Spinrad/Joan D. Vinge* • Elegy for Angels and Dogs/The Graveyard Heart, Walter Jon Williams/Roger Zelazny* • Fugue State/The Death of Doctor Island, John M. Ford/Gene Wolfe* • Press Enter ▓ / Hawksbill Station, John Varley/Robert Silverberg* • Eye for Eye/The Tunesmith, Orson Scott Card/Lloyd Biggle, Jr.*

forthcoming

SAMUEL R. DELANY

WE,

IN SOME STRANGE POWER'S EMPLOY, MOVE ON A RIGOROUS LINE

A TOM DOHERTY ASSOCIATES BOOK
NEW YORK

WE, IN SOME STRANGE POWER'S EMPLOY,
MOVE ON A RIGOROUS LINE

Copyright © 1968 by Mercury Press, Inc.
Copyright © 1990 by Samuel R. Delany

A Tor Book
Published by Tom Doherty Associates, Inc.
49 West 24th Street
New York, N.Y. 10010

Cover art by Wayne Barlowe

ISBN: 0-812-50983-8

First Tor edition: May 1990

Printed in the United States of America

0 9 8 7 6 5 4 3 2 1

—for R. Zelazny

ONE

Only the dark and her screaming.

First: sparks glint on her feet, and crack and snap, lighting rocks, dirt. Then no screams. She almost falls, whips erect. Silver leggings: Pop-pop-pop. Light laces higher, her arms are waving (trying to tell myself, "But she's dead already—"), and she weaves like a woman of white and silver paper, burning on the housing of the great ribbed cable exposed in the gully we'd torn from the earth.

"Thinking about your promotion?"

"Huh?" I looked up on Scott, who was poking at me with a freckled finger. Freckles, dime-sized and penny-colored, covered face, lips, arms, shoulders, got lost under the gold hair snarling his chest and belly. "What's it feel like

to be a section-devil? I've been opting for it two years now." Freckled fingers snapped. "Pass me up and take you!" He leaned back in his hammock, dug beneath his tool belt to scratch himself.

I shook my head. "No, something else. Something that happened awhile back. Nothing, really."

Night scoured our windows.

The Gila Monster sped.

Light wiped the panes and slipped away.

Scott suddenly sat up, caught his toes, and frowned. "Sometimes I think I'll spend the rest of my working life just a silver-suited line-demon, dancing along them damned strings." He pointed with his chin at the cross-section, sixteen-foot cable chart. "Come thirty-five, when I want to retire—and it's less than ten years off—what'll I be able to say? I did my job well?" He made a fist around the hammock edge. "I didn't do it well enough to make anything out of it." Hand open and up. "Some big black so-and-so like you comes along and three years later—section-devil!"

"You're a better demon than I am, Scott."

"Don't think I don't know it, either." Then he laughed. "No, let *me* tell *you*: a good demon doesn't necessarily make a good devil. The skills are different skills. The talents aren't the same. Hall, Blacky, you'd think, as your friend, I'd spare you. Say, when do you check out of this cabin? Gotta get used to somebody else's junk. Will you stay on at the old Monster here?"

"They said something about transferring me to Iguana. What with the red tape, it won't happen for a couple of weeks. I'll probably just give Mabel a hand till then. She gave me a room right over the tread motor. I complained about your snoring, and we agreed it would be an improvement."

That rated a swing; he just nodded.

I thought around for something to say and came up with: "You know I'm due an assistant, and I can choose—"

"Hell!" He flung himself back so I could only see his feet. (Underneath the hammock: one white woolen sock [gray toe], magazine, three wrenches.) "I'm no clerk. You have me running computers and keeping track of your confusion, filing reclamation plans and trying to hunt them out again—and all that for a drop in salary—"

"I wouldn't drop your salary."

"I'd go up the wall anyway."

"Knew that's what you'd say."

"Knew you'd make me say it."

"Well," I said, "Mabel asked me to come around to her office."

"Yeah. Sure." Release, relief. "Clever devil, Mabel. Hey. You'll be screening new applicants for whoever is gonna share my room now you been kicked upstairs. See if you can get a girl in here?"

"If I can." I grinned and stepped outside.

Gila Monster guts?

Three-quarters of a mile of corridors (much

less than some luxury ocean liners); two engine rooms that power the adjustable treads that carry us over land and sea; a kitchen, cafeteria, electrical room, navigation offices, office offices, tool repair shop, and cetera. With such in its belly, the Gila Monster crawls through the night (at about a hundred fifty k's cruising speed) sniffing along the great cables (courtesy the Global Power Commission) that net the world, web evening to night, dawn to day, and yesterday to morrow.

"Come in, Blacky," Mabel said at my knock.

She brushed back silver hair from her silver collar (the hair is natural) and closed the folder. "Seems we have a stop coming up just over the Canadian border."

"Pick up Scott's new roommate?"

"Power Cadet Susan Suyaki. Seventeen years old. Graduated third in her class last summer."

"Seventeen? Scott should like that."

"Wish she had some experience. The bright ones come out of school too snooty."

"I didn't."

"You still are."

"Oh, well. Scott prefers them with spirit."

"They're flying her in by helicopter to the site of our next job."

"Which line broke?"

"No break. It's a conversion."

I raised an eyebrow. "A rare experience for Miss Suyaki. I've only been through one, during my first couple of months on Salamander. That was a goodly while ago."

4

Mabel gave me a super-cynical-over-the-left-cheekbone. "You haven't *been* in the Power Corps a goodly while. You're just brilliant, that's all."

"It was a goodly while for *me*. Not all of us have had your thirty years experience, ma'am."

"I've always felt experience was vastly over-rated as a teacher." She started to clean her nails with a metal rule. "Otherwise, I would never have recommended you for promotion." Mabel is a fine devil.

"Thankee, thankee." I sat and looked at the ceiling map. "A conversion." Musing. "Salamander covered most of Mongolia. A little village in Tibet had to be connected up to the lines. We put cable through some of the damnedest rock. They were having an epidemic of some fever that gave you oozy blisters, and the medical crew was trying to set itself up at the same time. We worked twenty-four hours a day for three days, running lines, putting in outlets, and hooking up equipment. Three days to pull that primitive enclave of skin huts, caves, and lean-tos into the twenty-first century. Nothing resembling a heater in the whole place, and it was snowing when we got there."

Over joined fingertips Mabel bobbed her chin. "And to think, they'd been doddering along like that for the last three thousand years."

"Probably not much more than two hundred. The village had been established by refugees from the Sino-Japanese War. Still, I get your point."

"They were happy when you left?"

"They were happi-*er*," I said. "Still, you look at the maps—you trace cables over the world, and it's pretty hard to think there are still a few places that haven't been converted."

"I'm not as dreamy as you. Every couple of years Gila or Iguana stumbles over a little piece of the planet that's managed to fall through the net. They'll probably be turning them up a hundred years from now. People cling to their backwardness."

"Maybe you're—the border of *Canada*!"

"That is the longest take I've ever seen. Wake up, boy. Here I've been telling everybody how bright you are, recommending you for promotion—"

"Mabel, how can we have a conversion on the border of Canada? You convert villages in upper Anatolia, nameless little islands in the Indian Ocean—Tibet. There's no place you could lay another cable in the Americas. A town converted to Global Power along there?"

Mabel bobbed some more. "I don't like conversions. Always something messy. If everything went by the books, you'd think it would be one of our easiest maneuvers."

"You know me. I never go by the books."

She, musing this time: "True, doll. I still don't like 'em."

"The one I was telling you about in Tibet. We had a bad accident."

Mabel asked what it was with her eyebrows.

"A burning. Middle of the night, when some-

body had wandered down into the trough to troubleshoot one of the new connections. She was climbing up on the housing, when the power went on. Some sort of high amperage short. She went up like the proverbial moth."

Mabel stopped bobbing. "Who was she?"

"My wife."

"Oh." After a moment she said, "Burnings are bad. Hell of a waste of power, if nothing else. I wondered why you chose to room with Scott when you first came on the Gila Monster rather than Jane, Judy, or—"

"Julia was the young lady out for my tired brown body back then."

"You and your wife must have come straight out of the academy together. In your first year? Blacky, that's terrible. . . ."

"We had, that's right, and it was."

"I didn't know." Mabel looked adequately sincere.

"Don't tell me you didn't guess?"

"Don't joke . . . well, joke if you want." Mabel is a fine woman. "A conversion just over the Canadian border." She shook her head. "Blacky, we're going to have a problem, you and I."

"How so, ma'am?"

"Again: you are going to have a problem with me. I am going to have a problem with you."

"Pray, how, gentle lady?"

"You're a section-devil now. I'm a section-devil. You've been one for just under six hours. I've been one for just over sixteen years. But by

7

the books, we are in equal positions of authority."

"Fair maid," I said, "thou art off thy everloving nut."

"You're the one who doesn't go by the books. I do. Power of authority divided between two people doesn't work."

"If it makes you feel any better, I still consider you boss. You're the best boss I ever had too. Besides, I like you."

"Blacky—" she looked up at the skylight where the moon, outside the frame, still lit the tessellations—"there is something going on out there just across the border that I guess I know more about than you. You only know it's a conversion; and where it is, is odd. Let me warn you: you will want to handle it one way. I will want to handle it another."

"So we do it your way."

"Only I'm not so sure my way is best."

"Mabel—"

"Go, swarthy knight. We meet beyond the Canadian borders to do battle." She stood up looking very serious.

"If you say so."

"See you in the morning, Blacky."

I left the office, wondering at knights and days. Oh well, however, anyway: Scott was snoring, so I read until the rush of darkness outside was drifting gray.

TWO

The dawning sky (working top to bottom):
Sable, azure, gules—
—mountains dexter, sinister a hurst of oak,
lots of pines, a few maples. The Gila Monster
parked itself astride a foamy brook below a waterfall. I went outside on the balcony and got
showered as leaves sprinkled the stainless flank
of our great striding beast.

"Hello? Hey, hello!"

"Hi." I waved toward where she was climbing
down the—whoops! Into the water to her knee.
She squealed, climbed back up the rock, and
looked embarrassed.

"Cadet Suyaki?"

"Eh . . . yes, sir." She tried to rub her leg dry.
Canadian streams at dawn are cold.

I took off my shirt, made a ball, and flung it
to her. "Section-devil Jones." (She caught it.)
"Blacky'll do. We're pretty informal around
here."

"Oh . . . thank you." She lifted her silver legging, removed her boot to dry a very pretty ankle.

I gave the stairway a kick.

Clank-*chchchchc*-thud!

The steps unfolded, and the metal feet
stamped into pine needles. I went down to the
bank.

"Waiting long?"

She grinned. "Oh, I just got here."

And beyond the rocks there was a corroborative roar and snapping; a helicopter swung up through the trees.

Cadet Suyaki stood quickly and waved.

Somebody in the cockpit waved back till copper glare wiped him out.

"We saw you getting parked—" She looked down the length of Gila Monster.

I have said, or have I?

Cross an armadillo with a football field. Nurse the offspring on a motherly tank. By puberty: one Gila Monster.

"I'll be working under you?"

"Myself and Mabel Whyman."

She looked at me questioningly.

"Section-Devil Whyman—Mabel—is really in charge. I was just promoted from line-demon yesterday."

"Oh. Congratulations!"

"Hey, Blacky! Is that my new roommate?"

"That," I pointed at Scott, all freckled and golden, leaning over the rail, "is your pardner. You'll be rooming together."

Scott came down the steps, barefoot, denims torn off mid-thigh, tool belt full of calipers, meters, and insulation spools.

"Susan Suyaki," I announced, "Scott Mackelway."

She extended her hand. "I'm glad to meet—"

Scott put a big hand on each of little Miss Suyaki's shoulders. "So am I, honey. So am I."

"We'll be working very close together, won't

we?" asked Susan brightly. "I like that!" She squeezed one of his forearms. "Oh, I think this'll work out very well."

"Sure it will," Scott said. "I'm. . . ." Then I saw an open space on his ear pinken. "I sure hope it does."

"You two demons get over to the chameleon nest!"

Scott, holding Sue's hand, pointed up to the balcony. "That's Mabel. Hey, boss! We going any place I gotta put my shoes on?"

"Just scouting. Get going."

"We keep the chameleon over the port tread." Scott led Sue down the man-high links of the Monster's chain drive.

Thought: some twenty-four hours by, if Mabel had yelled, "You two demons . . ." the two demons would have been Scott and me.

She came, all silver, down the steps.

"You smile before the joust, Britomart?"

"Blacky, I'm turning into a dirty old woman." At the bottom step, she laid her forefinger on my chest, drew it slowly down my stomach and finally hooked my belt. "You're beautiful. And I'm not smiling, I'm leering."

I put my arm around her shoulder, and we walked the pine needles. She put her hands in her silver pockets. Hip on my thigh, shoulder knocking gently on my side, hair over my arm, she pondered the ferns and the oaks, the rocks and the water, the mountains and the flank of our Gila Monster couchant, the blaze of morning between the branches. "You're a devil. So

11

there are things I can say to you, ostensibly that would be meaningless to the others." She nodded ahead to where Scott and Sue were just disappearing around the three-meter hub.

"I await thy words most eagerly, Lady."

Mabel gestured at the Monster. "Blacky, do you know what the Monster, and the lines he prowls, really are?"

"I can tell you don't want an answer out of the book from your tone of voice, Miss Rules-and-Regulations."

"They're symbols of a way of life. Global Power Lines keep how many hundreds of thousands of refrigeration units functioning around the equator to facilitate food-storage; they've made the Arctic habitable. Cities like New York and Tokyo have cut population to a third of what they were a century ago. Back then, people used to be afraid they would crowd each other off the planet, would starve from lack of food. Yet the majority of the world was farming less than three percent of the arable land, and living on less than twenty percent of the world's surface. Global Power Lines meant that man could live any place on dry land he wanted, and a good number of places under the sea. National boundaries used to be an excuse for war; now they're only cartographical expedients. Riding in the Monster's belly, it's ironic that we are further from this way of life we're helping to maintain than most. But we still benefit."

"Of course."

"Have you ever asked yourself exactly how?"

"Education, leisure time," I suggested, "early and sliding retirements. . . ."

Mabel chuckled. "Oh, much more, Blacky. So much more. Men and women work together; our navigator, Faltaux, is one of the finest poets writing in French today, with an international reputation, and is still the best navigator I've ever had. And Julia, who keeps us so well fed and can pilot us quite as competently as I can, and is such a lousy painter, works with you and me and Faltaux and Scott on the same Maintenance Station. Or just the fact that you can move out of Scott's room one day and little Miss Suyaki can move in the next with an ease that would have amazed your great-great ancestors in Africa as much as mine in Finland. *That's* what this steel egg-crate means."

"Okay," I said. "I'm moved."

We came around the hub. Scott was heaving up the second door of the chameleon's garage and pointing out to Sue where the jack and the graphite can were kept.

"Some people," Mabel went on as I dropped my arm from her shoulder, "don't particularly like this way of life. Which is why we are about to attempt a conversion here on the Canadian border."

"A conversion?" Sue popped up. "Isn't that when you switch an area or a dwelling to Global—"

At which point Scott swung at Mabel. He caught her upside the head. She yelled and went staggering into the leaves.

I jumped back, and Sue did a thing with her Adam's apple.

Something went *Nnnnnnnnnn* against the hub, then chattered away through the ferns. Ferns fell.

"Look!" Sue cried.

I was staring at the eight-inch scratch in the Gila Monster's very hard hide, at about the level where Mabel's carotid had been a moment back.

But across the water, scrambling up the rocks, was a yellow-headed kid wearing a little less than Scott.

Sue ran through the weeds and picked up the blade. "Were they trying to *kill* somebody?"

Mabel shrugged. "You're Cadet Suyaki? We're going to explore the conversion site. Dear me, that looks vicious."

"I used to hunt with a bolo," Sue said warily. "At home. But I've never even *seen* one of these . . . ?" Two blades were bolted in a twisted cross, all four prongs sharpened.

"My first too. Hope it's my last." Mabel looked around the clearing. "Am I ever optimistic. Pleased to meet you, Suyaki. Well, come on. Crank up Nelly. And for Pete's sake, let's get *in.*"

The chameleon, ten feet long, is mostly transparent plastic, which means you can see sea, sunset, or forest right through.

Scott drove with Mabel beside him.

Me and Sue sat in back.

We found the chewed-up asphalt of an old road and crawled right along up the mountain.

14

"Where are . . . we going, exactly?" Sue asked.

"Honey," Mabel said, "I'll let you know when we get there." She put the throwing blade in the glove compartment with a grunt. Which does a lot of good with transparent plastic.

THREE

Sue leaned against the door. "Oh, look! Look down!"

We'd wound high enough and looped back far enough on the abominable road so that you could gaze down through the breaks; beyond the trees and rocks you could see the Gila Monster. It still looked big.

"Eh . . . look up," suggested Scott and slowed the chameleon. A good-sized tree had come up by the roots and fallen across the road.

The man standing in front of it was very dirty. The kid behind, peering through the Medusa of roots, was the one who had tried to decapitate Mabel.

"What . . . are they?" Sue whispered.

"Scott and Sue, you stay right here and keep the door open so we can get in fast. Blacky, we go on up."

The man's hair, under the grease, was brass-colored.

Some time ago his left cheek had been opened up, then sewn so clumsily you could see the cross-stitching. The lobe of his left ear was a rag of flesh. His sleeve-ripped shirt hung but-

15

tonless and too short to tuck in, even if he'd had a mind to. A second welt plowed an inch furrow through chest hair, wrecked his right nipple, and disappeared under his collar.

As we came up, Mabel took the lead. I overtook her; she gave me a faint-subtle-nasty and stepped ahead again.

He was a hard guy, but the beginning of a gut was showing over the double bar and chain contraption he used to fasten his studded belt. At first I thought he was wearing mismatched shoes: one knee-high, scuffed, and crack-soled boot. The other foot was bare, a length of black chain around the ankle, two toes, little and middle, gone.

I looked back at his face to see his eyes come up to mine.

Well, I was still sans shirt; back at the chameleon Sue's pants leg was still rolled up. Mabel was the only one of us proofed neat and proper.

He looked at Mabel. He looked at me. He looked at Mabel. Then he bent his head and said, "Rchht-*ah*-pt, what are you doing up here, huh?" That first word produced a yellow oyster about eight inches north of Mabel's boot toe, six south of his bare one. His head came up, the lower lip glistening and hanging away from long, yellow teeth.

"Good morning." I offered my hand. "We're ..." (He looked at it.) "... surveying."

He took his thumb from his torn pocket; we shook. A lot of grease, a lot of callus, it was the

hand of a very big man who had bitten his nails since he was a very small boy.

"Yeah? What are you surveying?"

He wore a marvelous ring.

"We're from Global Power Commission."

Take a raw, irregular nugget of gold—

"Figured. I saw your machine down the road."

—a nugget three times the size either taste or expediency might allow a ring—

"We've had reports that the area is underpowered for the number of people living here."

—punch a finger-sized hole, so that most of the irregularities are on one side—

"Them bastards down in Hainesville probably registered a complaint. Well, we don't live in Hainesville. Don't see why it should bother them."

—off center in the golden crater place an opal, big as his—as *my* thumbnail—

"We have to check it out. Inadequate power doesn't do anybody any good."

—put small diamonds in the tips of the three prongs that curved to cage the opal—

"You think so?"

—and in the ledges and folds of bright metal capping his enlarged knuckle, bits of spodumene, pyrope, and spinel, all abstract, all magnificent.

"Look, mister," I said, "the Hainesville report says there are over two dozen people living on this mountain. The power commission doesn't register a *single* outlet."

He slipped his hands into his back pockets. "Don't believe I have seen any, now you mention it."

Mabel said, "The law governs how much power and how many outlets must be available and accessible to each person. We'll be laying lines up here this afternoon and tomorrow morning. We're not here to make trouble. We don't want to find any."

"What makes you think you might?"

"Well, your friend over there already tried to cut my head off."

He frowned, glanced back through the roots. Suddenly he leaned back over the trunk and took a huge swipe. "Get out of here, Pitt!"

The kid squeaked. The face flashed in the roots (lank hair, a spray of acne across flat cheek and sharp chin), and jangling at her hip was a hank of throwing blades. She disappeared into the woods.

As the man turned, I saw, tattooed on the bowl of his shoulder, a winged dragon, coiled about and gnawing at a swastika.

Mabel ignored the whole thing:

"We'll be finished down the mountain this morning and will start bringing the lines up here this afternoon."

He gave half a nod—lowered his head and didn't bring it up—and that was when it dawned on me we were doing this thing wrong.

"We do want to do this easily," I said. "We're not here to make problems for you."

His hands crawled from his knees back to his waist.

"You can help us by letting people know that. If anyone has any questions about what we're doing, or doesn't understand something, they can come and ask for me. I'm Section-Devil Jones. Just ask for Blacky down at the Gila Monster."

"My name's Roger ..." followed by something Polish and unpronounceable that began with Z and ended in Y. "If you have problems, you can come to me. Only I ain't saying I can do anything."

Good exit line. But Roger stayed where he was. And Mabel beside me was projecting stark disapproval.

"Where do most of the folks around here live?" I asked, to break the silence.

He nodded up. "On High Haven."

"Is there somebody in charge, a mayor or something like that I could talk to?"

Roger looked at me like he was deciding where I'd break easiest if he hit. "That's why I'm down here talking to you."

"You?" I didn't ask. What I *did* say was: "Then perhaps we could go up and see the community. I'd like to see how many people are up there, perhaps suggest some equipment, determine where things have to be done."

"You want to visit on High?"

"If we might."

He made a fist and scratched his neck with the prongs of his ring. "All right." He gestured

19

back toward the chameleon. "You can't get that any further up the road."

"Will you take us, then?"

He thought awhile. "Sure." Then he let a grin open over the yellow cage of teeth. "Get you back down too." Small victory.

"Just a moment," Mabel said, "while we go back and tell the driver."

We strolled to the chameleon.

"You don't sound very happy with my attempt to make peace."

"Have I said a word?"

"*Just* what I mean. Can you imagine how these people live, Mabel, if Roger there is the head of the Chamber of Commerce?"

"I can imagine."

"He looks as bad as any of those villagers in Tibet. Did you *see* the little girl? This, in the middle of the twenty-first century!"

". . . just over the Canadian border. Scott," Mabel said, "take me and Sue back down to the Monster. If you are not back by noon, Blacky, we will come looking for you."

"Huh? You mean you're not going with me? Look," I told Scott's puzzled frown, "don't worry, I'll be back. Sue, can I have my shirt?"

"Oh, I'm terribly sorry! Here you are. It may be damp—"

"Mabel, if we did go up there together—"

"Blacky, running this operation with two devils admittedly presents problems. Running it with none at all is something else entirely.

You're a big devil now. You know what you're doing. I even know. I just think you're crazy."

"*Ma*-bel—"

"On up there with you! And sow as much goodwill as you can. If it avoids one tenth the problems I know we're going to have in the next twelve hours, I will be eternally grateful."

Then Mabel, looking determined, and Sue and Scott, looking bewildered, climbed into the chameleon.

"Oh." She leaned out the door. "Give this back to them." She handed me the throwing blade. "See you by noon." The chameleon swayed off down the road. I put my shirt on, stuck the blade in my belt, and walked back to Roger.

He glanced at it, and we both thought nasty-nasty-evilness at one another. "Come on." He climbed over the tree. I climbed over after.

Parked behind the trunk was an old twin-turbo pteracycle. Roger lifted it by one black and chrome bat-form wing. The chrome was slightly flaked. With one hand he grasped the steering shaft and twisted the choke ring gently. The other hand passed down the wing with the indifference we use to mask the grosser passions. "Hop on my broomstick and I'll take you up to where the angels make their Haven." He grinned.

And I understood many things.

So:

21

Small Essay

on a phenomenon current some fifty years back when the date had three zeroes. (Same time as the first cables were being laid and demons were beginning to sniff about the world in silver armor, doctoring breaks, repairing relays, replacing worn housings. Make the fancy sociological connections, please.) That's when pteracycles first became popular as a means of short-(and sometimes not so short-)range transportation. Then they were suddenly taken up by a particularly odd set of asocials. Calling themselves individualists, they moved in veritable flocks; dissatisfied with society, they wracked the ages for symbols from the most destructive epochs: skull and bones, fasces, swastika, and guillotine. They were accused of the most malicious and depraved acts, sometimes with cause, sometimes without. They took the generic name of angels (Night's Angels, Red Angels, Hell's Angels, Bloody Angels, one of these lifted from a similar cult popular another half century before. But then most of their mythic accouterments were borrowed). The common sociological explanation: they were a reaction to population decentralization, the last elements of violence in a neutral world. Psychological: well, after all, what does a pteracycle look like?—two round cam-turbines on which you sit between the wings, then this six-foot metal shaft sprouting up between your legs that you steer with (hence the sobriquet "broomstick") and nothing else but goggles between you and the sky.

You figure it. Concluding remarks: angels were a product of the turn of the century. But nobody's heard anything serious about them for thirty years. They went out with neon buttons, the common cold, and transparent vinyl jockey shorts. Oh, the teens of *siècle* twenty-one saw some dillies! The End.

I climbed on the back seat. Roger got on the front, toed one of the buttons on the stirrup (for any fancy flying you have to do some pretty fast button-pushing; ergo, the bare foot), twisted the throttle ring, and lots of leaves shot up around my legs. The cycle skidded up the road, bounced twice on cracks, then swerved over the edge. We dropped ten feet before we caught the draft and began the long arc out and up. Roger flew without goggles.

The wind over his shoulder carried a smell I first thought was the machine. Imagine a still that hasn't bathed for three months. He flew *very* well.

"How many people are there in High Haven?" I called.

"What?"

"I said, how many people are there in—"

"About twenty-seven!"

We curved away from the mountain, curved back.

The Gila Monster flashed below, was gone behind rocks. The mountain turned, opened a rocky gash.

At the back of the gorge, vaulting the stream

23

that plummeted the mountain's groin, someone had erected a mansion. It was a dated concrete and glass monstrosity from the late twentieth century (pre-power lines). Four terraced stories were cantilevered into the rock. Much of the glass was broken. Places that had once been garden had gone wild with vine and brush. A spectacular metal stairway wound from the artificial pool by the end of the roadway that was probably the same one we'd ridden with the chameleon, from porch to porch, rust-blotched like a snake's back.

The house still had much stolid grandeur. Racked against a brick balustrade were maybe twenty pteracycles (what better launch than the concrete overhang, railing torn away). One cycle was off the rack. A guy was on his knees before it, the motor in pieces around him. A second, fists on hips, was giving advice.

A third guy shielded his eyes to watch us. A couple of others stopped by the edge of the pool. One was the girl, Pitt, who had been down with Roger before.

"High Haven?"

"What?" Pteracycles are loud.

"Is that High Haven?"

"Yeah." We glided between the rocks, skimmed foaming boulders, rose toward glass and concrete. Cement rasped beneath the runners, and we jounced to a stop.

A couple of guys stepped from a broken window. A couple more came up the steps. Someone looking from the upper porch disappeared,

to return a moment later with five others, another girl among them.

There was a lot of dirt, a lot of hair, a number of earrings. (I counted four more torn ears; I'd avoid fights if I were going to wear my jewelry that permanent). A kid with much red hair—couldn't quite make a beard yet—straddled the cycle rack. He pushed back the flap of his leather jacket to scratch his bare belly with black nails. The dragon on his chest beat its wings about the twisted cross.

I got off the cycle left, Roger right.

Someone said: "Who's that?"

A few of the guys glanced over their shoulders, then stepped aside so we could see.

She stood by the dawn-splashed hem of glass at the side of the broken wall-window.

"He's from the Global Power Commission." Roger shoved a thumb at me. "They're parked down the mountain."

"You can tell him to go back to hell where he came from."

She wasn't young. She was beautiful though.

"We don't need anything he's selling."

The others mumbled, shuffled.

"Shut it," Roger said. "He's not selling anything."

I stood there feeling uncomfortably silver, but wondering that I'd managed to win over Roger.

"That's Fidessa," he said.

She stepped through the window.

Wide, high facial bones, a dark mouth and darker eyes. I want to describe her hair as am-

ber, but it was an amber so dark only direct sunlight caught its reds. The morning fell full on it; it spread her shoulders. Her hands were floured, and she smeared white on her hips as she came toward me.

"Fidessa?" All right. I'm not opposed to reality imitating art if it doesn't get in the way.

"He's okay," Roger said in response to her look.

"Yeah?"

"Yeah. Get out of the way." He shoved her. She nearly collided with one of the men, who just stepped out of the way in time. She still gave the poor guy a withering *noli me tangere* stare. Kept her stuff, too.

"You want to see the place?" Roger said and started in. I followed.

Someone who looked like he was used to it picked up Roger's cycle and walked it to the rack.

Fidessa came up beside us as we stepped into the house.

"How long has this bunch been here?" I asked.

"There's been angels on High for forty years. They come; they go. Most of this bunch has been here all summer."

We crossed a room where vandals, time, and fire had left ravage marks. The backs of the rooms had been cut into the rock. One wall, wood-paneled, had become a palimpsest of scratched names and obscenities: old motors

and motor parts, a pile of firewood, rags, and chains.

"We don't want power up here," Fidessa said. "We don't need it." Her voice was belligerent and intense.

"How do you survive?"

"We hunt," Roger said as the three of us turned down a stone stairwell. The walls at the bottom flickered. "There's Hainesville about ten miles from here. Some of us go over there and work when we have to."

"Work it over a little too?" (Roger's mouth tightened.) "When you have to?"

"When we have to."

I could smell meat cooking. And bread.

I glanced at Fidessa's powdered hips. They rocked with her walking: I didn't look away.

"Look." I stopped three steps from the doorway. "About the power installation here." Light over my uniform deviled the bottom of my vision.

Roger and Fidessa looked.

"You've got over two dozen people here, and you say there have been people here for forty years? How do you cook? What do you do for heat in winter? Suppose you have medical emergencies? Forget the law. It's made for you; not us."

"Go to hell," Fidessa said and started to turn away. Roger pulled her back by the shoulder.

"I don't care how you live up here," I said because at least Roger was listening. "But you've got winter sitting on your doorstop. You

use liquid fuel for your broomsticks. You could have them converted to battery and run them off rechargeable cells for a third of the cost."

"Storage cells still give you about a hundred and fifty miles less than a full liquid tank."

Fidessa looked disgusted and started downstairs again. I think Roger was losing patience because he turned after her. I followed again.

The lower room was filled with fire.

Chains and pulley apparatus hung from the ceiling. Two furnaces were going. Two pit fires had been dug into the floor. The ceiling was licked across with inky tongues. Hot air brushed back and forth across my face; the third brush left it sweaty.

I looked for food.

"This is our forge." Roger picked up a small sledge and rattled it against a sheet of corrugated iron leaning on the wall. "Danny, come out here!"

Barefoot, soot-smeared, the smears varnished with sweat: bellows and hammers had pulled the muscles taut, chiseled and defined them, so that each sat on his frame apart. Haircut and bath admitted, he would have been a fine-looking kid—twenty, twenty-five? He came forward knuckling his left eye. The right was that strange blue-gray that always seems to be exploding when it turns up (so rarely) in swarthy types like him.

"Hey there! What you doing?" Roger grimaced at me. "He's nearly deaf."

Danny dropped his fist from his face and motioned us into the back.

And I caught my breath.

What he'd been rubbing wasn't an eye at all. Scarred, crusted, then the crust broken and drooling; below his left eyebrow was only a leaking sore.

We followed Danny between the fires and anvils to a worktable at the back. Piles of throwing blades (I touched the one in my belt) were at varied stages of completion. On the pitted boards among small hammers, punches, and knives, were some lumps of gold, a small pile of gems, and three ingots of silver. About the jeweler's anvil lay earrings, and a buckle with none of the gems set.

"This is what you're working on now?" Roger picked up the buckle in greasy fingers already weighted with gold.

I bent to see, then pointed from the buckle to Roger's ring, and looked curious. (Why are we always quiet or shouting before the deaf?) Roger nodded.

"Danny does a lot of stuff for us. He's a good machinist too. We're all pretty good turbo mechanics, but Danny here can do real fine stuff. Sometimes we fly him over to Hainesville, and he works there."

"Another source of income?"

"Right."

Just then Pitt came between the flames. She held half a loaf of bread. "Hey, Danny!" in a

voice for the deaf, "I brought you some—" saw us and stopped.

Danny looked up, grinned, and circled the girl's shoulder with one arm, took the bread in the other hand, and bit.

His smile reflected off Pitt's.

The elastic fear loosened on her face as she watched the one-eyed smith chewing crust. She was very close to pretty then.

I was glad of that.

Danny turned back to the bench, Pitt's shoulder still tucked under his arm. He fingered the rings, found a small one for her, and she pulled forward with, "Oh . . ." and the gold flickered in her palm. The smile moved about her face like flame. (The throwing blades clinked on her hip.) Silent Danny had the rapt look of somebody whose mind was bouncing off the delight he could give others.

Fidessa said: "Have they got all of the first batch out of the ovens?" She looked at the bread and actually snarled. Then she sucked her teeth, turned, and marched away.

"Say," I asked Pitt, "do you like it up here?"

She dropped the ring, looked at me; then all the little lines of fear snapped back.

I guess Danny hadn't heard me, but he registered Pitt's discomfort. As he looked between us, his expression moved toward bewildered anger.

"Come on." Roger surprised me with a cuff on the shoulder. "Leave the kids alone. Get out

of here." I was going to object to being pushed, but I guess Roger just pushed people. We left.

"Hey," Roger said, watching his feet as he walked, "I want to explain something to you." We left the fires. "We don't want any power up here."

"That has come across." I tried to sound as sincere as he did. "But there is the law." Sincerity is my favorite form of belligerence.

Roger stopped in front of the window (unbroken here), put his hands in his back pockets, and watched the stream spit down the gorge.

It was, I realized, the same stream the Gila Monster was parked across a mile below.

"You know I'm new at this job, Blacky," he said after a while. "I've just been archangel a couple of weeks. The only reason I took over the show is because I had some ideas on how to do it better than the guy before me. One of my ideas was to run it with as little trouble as possible."

"Who was running it before?"

"Sam was archangel before I was, and Fidessa was head cherub. They ran the business up here, and they ran it hard."

"Sam?"

"Take a whole lot of mean and pour it into a hide about three times as ugly as mine: Sam. He put out Danny's eye. When we get hold of a couple of cases of liquor, we have some pretty wild times up here. Sam came down to the forge to fool around. He heated up one end of a pipe and started swinging it at people. He liked to see them

31

jump and holler. That's the kind of mean he was. Danny doesn't like people fooling around with his tools and things anyway. Sam got after Pitt, and Danny rushed him. So Sam stuck the hot pipe into Danny's head." Roger flexed his thumbs. "When I saw that, I realized I was going to have to do something. We rumbled about two weeks ago." He laughed and dropped his hands. "There was a battle in Haven that day!"

"What happened?"

He looked at the water. "You know the top porch of Haven? I threw him off the top porch onto the second. Then I came down and hurled him headlong off onto the bottom one." He pointed out the window. "Then I came down and threw him into the river. He limped around until I finally told the guys to take a couple of flaming torches and run him down the rocks where I couldn't see him no more." Behind his back now he twisted his ring. "I can't see him. Maybe he made it to hell . . . or Hainesville."

"Did . . . eh, Fidessa go along with the promotion?"

"Yeah." He brought his hands before him. Light struck and struck in the irregularities of metal. "I don't think I would have tried for the job if she hadn't. She's a lot of woman."

"Kill the king and take the queen."

"I took Fidessa first. Then I had to . . . kill the king. That's the way things go in Haven."

"Roger?"

He didn't look at me.

"Look, you've got a kid back there at the anvil

32

who needs a doctor. You say he's a good part of your bread and butter. And you let him walk around with a face like that? What *are* you trying to do?"

"Sam used to say we were trying to live long enough to show the bastards how mean we could be. I say we're just trying to live."

"Suppose Danny's eye infection decides to spread? I'm not casting moral aspersions just to gum up the works. I'm asking if you're even doing what you want to." (He played with his ring.) "So you've avenged Danny; you won the fair damsel. What about that infection—"

Roger turned on me. His scar twisted on his cheek, and lines of anger webbed his forehead. "You really think we didn't try to get him to a doctor? We took him to Hainesville, then we took him to Kingston, then back to Hainesville and finally out to Edgeware. We carried that poor screaming half-wit all over the night." He pointed back among the fires. "Danny grew up in an institute, and you get him anywhere near a city when he's scared, and he'll try to run away. We couldn't get him in to a doctor."

"He didn't run away from here when his eye was burned."

"He lives here. He's got a place to do the few things he can do well. He's got a woman. He's got food and people to take care of him. The business with Sam, I don't even think he understood what happened. When you're walking through a forest and a tree falls on you and breaks your leg, you don't run away from the

forest. Danny didn't understand that he was more important in Haven than big Sam with all his orders and bluster and beat-you-to-a-pulp if you look at him wrong: that's why Sam had to hurt him. But you try to explain that to Danny." He gestured at the fire. "*I* understood though." As he gestured, his eye caught on the points and blades of the ring. Again he stopped to twist it. "Danny made this for Sam. I took it off him on the bottom porch."

"I still want to know what's going to happen to Danny."

Roger frowned. "When we couldn't get him into a doctor's office in Edgeware, we finally went into town, woke up the doctor there at two in the morning, made him come outside the town and look at him there. The doc gave him a couple of shots of antibiotics and some salve to put on it, and Pitt makes sure he puts it on every day too. The doc said not to bandage it because it heals better in the air. We're bringing him back to check it next week. What the hell do you think we are?" He didn't sound like he wanted an answer. "You said you wanted to look around. Look. When you're finished, I'll take you back down, and you tell them we don't want no power lines up here!" He shook his jeweled finger at me with the last six words.

I walked around Haven awhile (pondering as I climbed the flickering stair that even the angels in Haven have their own spot of hell), trying to pretend I was enjoying the sun and the breeze, looking over the shoulders of the guys

working on their cycles. People stopped talking when I passed. Whenever I turned, somebody looked away. Whenever I looked at one of the upper porches, somebody moved away.

I had been walking twenty long minutes when I finally came into a room to find Fidessa, smiling.

"Hungry?"

She held an apple in one hand and in the other half a loaf of that brown bread, steaming.

"Yeah." I came and sat beside her on the split-log bench.

"Honey?" in a can rusted around the edge with a kitchen knife stuck in it.

"Thanks." I spread some on the bread, and it went running and melting into all those little air bubbles like something in Danny's jewelry furnace. And I hadn't had breakfast. The apple was so crisp and cold it hurt my teeth. And the bread was warm.

"You're being very nice."

"It's too much of a waste of time the other way. You've come up here to look around. All right. What have you seen?"

"Fidessa," I said, after a silent while in which I tried to fit her smile with her last direct communication with me ("Go to hell," it was?) and couldn't. "I am *not* dense. I do *not* disapprove of you people coming up here to live away from the rest of the world. The chains and leather bit is not exactly my thing, but I haven't seen anybody here under sixteen, so you're all old enough to vote: in my book that means run your

own lives. I could even say this way of life opens pathways to the more mythic and elemental hooey of mankind. I have heard Roger, and I have been impressed, yea, even moved, by how closely his sense of responsibility resembles my own. I too am new at my job. I still don't understand this furor over half a dozen power outlets. We come peacefully; we'll be out in a couple of hours. Leave us the key, go make a lot of noise over some quiet hamlet, and shake up the locals. We'll lock up when we go and stick it under the door mat. You won't even know we've been here."

"Listen, line-demon—"

An eighty-seven-year-old granny of mine, who had taken part in the Detroit race riots in nineteen sixty-nine, must have used that same tone to a bright-eyed civil rights worker in the middle of the gunfire who, three years later, became my grandfather: "Listen, white-boy. . . ." Now I understood what granny had been trying to get across with her anecdote.

"—you don't know what's going on up here. You've wandered around for half an hour, and nobody but me and Roger have said a thing to you. What is it you think you understand?

"Please, not demon. Devil."

"All you've seen is a cross-section of a process. Do you have any idea what was here five, or fifteen, years ago? Do you know what will be here five years from now? When I came here for the first time, almost ten years back—"

"You and Sam?"

Four thoughts passed behind her face, none of which she articulated.

"When Sam and me first got here, there were as many as a hundred and fifty angels at a time roosting here. Now there's twenty-one."

"Roger said twenty-seven."

"Six left after Sam and Roger rumbled. Roger thinks they're going to come back. Yoggy might. But not the others."

"And in five years?"

She shook her head. "Don't you understand? You don't have to kill us off. We're dying."

"We're not trying to kill you."

"You are."

"When I get down from here, I'm going to do quite a bit of proselytizing. Devil often speak with"—I took another bite of bread—"honeyed tongue. Might as well use it on Mabel." I brushed crumbs from my shining lap.

She shook her head, smiling sadly. "No." I wish women wouldn't smile sadly at me. "You are kind, handsome, perhaps even good." They always bring that up too. "And you are out to kill us."

I made frustrated noises.

She held up the apple.

I bit; she laughed.

She stopped laughing.

I looked up.

There in the doorway Roger looked a mite puzzled.

I stood. "You want to run me back down the mountain?" I asked with brusque ingenuous-

ness. "I can't promise you anything. But I'm going to see if I can't get Mabel to sort of forget
this job and take her silver-plated juggernaut
somewhere else."

"You just do ... this thing," Roger said.
"Come on."

While Roger was cutting his pteracyle out
from the herd, I glanced over the edge.

At the pool, Pitt had coaxed Danny in over his
knees. It couldn't have been sixty-five degrees
out. But they were splashing and laughing like
mud puppies from, oh, some warmer clime.

FOUR

A Gila Monster rampant?
Watch:
Six hydraulic lifts with cylinders thick as oil
drums adjust the suspension up another five
feet to allow room for blade work. From the
"head" the "plow," slightly larger than the skull
of a Triceratops, chuckles down into the dirt,
digs down into the dirt. What chuckled before,
roars. Plates on the side slide back.

Then Mabel, with most of her office, emerges
on a telescoping lift to peer over the demons'
shoulders with telephoto television.

The silver crew itself scatters across the pine
needles like polished bearings. The monster
hunkers backward, dragging the plow (angled
and positioned by one of the finest contempo-

rary poets of the French language): a trough two dozen feet wide and deep is opened upon the land. Two mandibles extend now, with six-foot wire brushes that rattle around down there, clearing off the top of the ribbed housing of a sixteen-foot cable. Two demons (Ronny and Ann) guide the brushes, staking worn ribs, metering for shorts in the higher frequency levels. When the silver worm has been bared a hundred feet, side cabinets open, and from over the port treads the crane swings out magnetic grapples.

One of the straightest roads in the world runs from Leningrad to Moscow. The particular czar involved, when asked for his suggestion as to just where the road should run, surprised architects and chancellors by taking a rule and scribing a single line between the cities. "There," he said, or its Russian equivalent. What with Russia being what it was in the mid-eighteenth century, there the road was built.

Except in some of the deeper Pacific trenches and certain annoying Himalayan passes, the major cables and most of the minor ones were laid out much the same way. The only time a cable ever bends sharp enough to see is when a joint is put in. We were putting in a joint.

Inside, demons (Julia, Bill, Frank, Dimitri) are readying the clip, a U of cable fifteen feet from bend to end. On those ends are very complicated couplings. They check those couplings very carefully, because the clip carries all that juice around the gap while the joint is being inserted.

The cranes start to squeal as, up in her tower, Mabel presses the proper button. The clip rises from the monster's guts, swings over the gleaming rib with Scott hanging onto the rope and riding the clip like some infernal surfer.

Frank and Dimitri come barreling from between the tread rollers to join Sue outside, so that the half-circle clips slip over the cable right on the chalk mark. Then Scott slides down to dance on the line with a ratchet, Sue with another. On each end of the clip they drive down the contacts that sink to various depths in the cable.

Frank: "She uses that thing pretty well."

Dimitri: "Maybe they're teaching them something in the academy after all these years?"

Frank: "She's just showing off because she's new—hey, Sue? Do you think she'd go after a neck tourniquet if we sent her?"

The eight-foot prong goes down to center core. Sixty thousand volts there. The seven-foot six-inch goes to the stepper ground. That's a return for a three-wire high voltage line that boosts you up from the central core to well over three hundred thousand volts. Between those two, you can run all the utilities for a city of a couple or six million. Next prong takes you down to general high-frequency utility power. Then low-frequency same. There's a layer of communcations circuits next that lets you plug into a worldwide computer system: I mean if you ever need a worldwide computer. Then the local antennae for radio and TV broadcasts. Then

all the check circuits to make sure that all the inner circuits are functioning. Then smaller antennae that broadcast directly to Gila Monster and sibling the findings of the check circuits. And so forth. And so on. For sixteen feet.

Scott's ratchet clicks on the bolt of the final prong (he let Sue beat him—he will say—by one connection), and somebody waves up at Mabel, who has discovered they're a minute and a half behind schedule and worries about these things.

Another crane is lowering the double blade. Teeth ratch, and sparks whiten their uniforms. Demons squint and move back.

Dimitri and Scott are already rolling the connecting disk on the sledge to the rim of the trough ("Hey, Sue! Watch it, honey. This thing only weighs about three hundred pounds!"

("I bet she don't make a hundred and ten.")

A moment later the blade pulls away, and the section of cable is lifted and tracked down the monster, and the whole business slips into the used-blade compartment.

The joint, which has the connections to take taps from the major cable so we can string the lines of power to Haven itself, is rolled and jimmied into place. Ratchets again. This time the whole crew screws the lugs to the housing.

And Mabel sighs and wipes her pale, moist brow, having gotten through the operation without a major blackout anywhere in the civilized world—nothing shorted, casualties nil, injuries same. All that is left is for the U to be

removed so that things start flowing again. And there's hardly anything that can go wrong now.

Roger got me back just as they were removing the U. I came jogging down the rocks, waved to people, bopped on up the stairs, and played through the arteries of the beast. I came out on the monster's back, shielding my eyes against the noon.

The shadow of Mabel's office swung over me. I started up the ladder on the side of the lift, and moments later poked my head through the trapdoor.

"Hey, Mabel! Guess what's up on High Haven."

I don't think she was expecting me. She jumped a little. "What?"

"A covey of pteracycle angels, straight from the turn of the century. Tattoos, earrings, leather jackets and all—actually I don't think most of them can afford jackets. They're pretty scroungy."

Mabel frowned. "That's nice."

I hoisted to sitting position. "They're not really bad sorts. Eccentric, yes. I know you just got through connecting things up. But what say we roll up all our extension cords and go someplace else?"

"You are out of your mind." Her frown deepened.

"Naw. Look, they're just trying to do their thing. Let's get out of here."

"Nope."

"They look on this whole business as an attempt to wipe them—why not?"

"Because I want to wipe them out."

"Huh? Now don't tell me you were buzzed by angels when you were a little girl and you've carried feud fodder ever since."

"Told you we were going to argue, Blacky." She turned around in her chair. "The last time I had a conversion, it was a vegetarian cult that had taken refuge in the Rockies. Ate meat only once a year on the eve of the autumnal equinox. I will never forget the look on that kid's face. The first arrow pinned his shirt to the trunk of an oak—"

"Happy Halloween, St. Sebastian. *Ehhh!* But these aren't cannibals," I said, "Mabel."

"The conversion before that was a group of utopian socialists who had set up camp in the Swiss Alps. I don't think I could ever trace a killing directly to them—I'm sorry, I'm not counting the three of my men who got it when the whole business broke out into open fighting. But they made the vegetarians look healthy: at least they got it out of their systems. The one before that—"

"Mabel—"

"I assume you're interrupting me because you've gotten my point."

"You were talking about ways of life before. Hasn't it occurred to you that there is more than one way of life possible?"

"That is too asinine for me even to bother answering. Get up off the floor."

I got up.

"If we are going to begin our argument with obvious banalities, consider these: hard work does not hurt the human machine. That's what it is made for. But to work hard simply to remain undernourished, or to have to work harder than you're able so that someone else can live well while you starve, or to have no work at all and have to watch yourself and others starve—this is disastrous to the human machine. Subject any statistically meaningful sample of people to these situations, and after a couple of generations you will have wars, civil and sovereign, along with all the neuroses that such a *Weltanschauung* produces."

"You get an A for obviousness."

"The world being the interrelated mesh that it is, two hundred million people starving in Asia had an incalculable effect on the psychology and sociology of the two hundred million overfed, overleisured North Americans during the time of our grandparents."

"B for banality."

"Conclusion—"

"For which you automatically get a C."

"—there has not been a war in forty years. There were only six murders in New York City last year. Nine in Tokyo. The world has a ninety-seven percent literacy rate. Eighty-four percent of the world population is at least bilingual. Of all the political and technological machinations that have taken place in the last century to cause this, Global Power Lines were probably

the biggest single factor. Because suddenly people did not have to work to starve. That problem was alleviated, and the present situation has come about in the time it takes a child to become a grandparent. The generation alive when Global Power began was given the time to raise an interesting bunch of neurotics for a second generation, and they had the intelligence and detachment to raise their bunch healthy enough to produce us."

"We've gone about as far as we can go?"

"Don't be snide. My point is simply that in a world where millions were being murdered by wars and hundreds of thousands by less efficient means, there was *perhaps* some justification for saying about any given injustice, 'What can I do?' But that's not this world. Perhaps we know too much about our grandparents' world so that we expect things to be like that. But when the statistics are what they are today, one boy shot full of arrows to a tree is a very different matter."

"What I saw up there—"

"—bespoke violence, brutality, unwarranted cruelty from one person to another, and if not murder, the potential for murder at every turn. Am I right?"

"But it's a life they've chosen! They have their own sense of honor and responsibility. You wouldn't go see, Mabel. I did. It's not going to harm—"

"Look, Teak-head! Somebody tried to kill *me*

this morning with that thing you've still got in your belt!"

"Mabel—!" which exclamation had nothing to do with our argument.

She snatched up the microphone, flicked the button. "Scott, what the hell are you doing!" Her voice, magnified by the loudspeakers, rolled over the plates and dropped among demons.

What Scott Had Done:

He'd climbed on the U to ride it back up into the monster. With most of the prongs ratcheted out, he had taken a connector line (probably saying to Sue first, "Hey, I bet you never seen this before!") and tapped the high voltage and stuck it against the metal housing. There's only a fraction of an ampere there, so it wasn't likely to hurt anything. The high voltage effect in the housing causes a brush discharge the length of the exposed cable. Very impressive. Three-foot sparks crackling all over, and Scott grinning, and all his hair standing up on end.

A hedge of platinum—

A river of diamonds—

A jeweled snake—

What is dangerous about it and why Mabel was upset is (One) if something does go wrong with that much voltage, it is going to be more than serious. (Two) The U clip's connected to the (Bow!) gig-crane; the gig-crane's connected to the (Poo!) crane-house; the crane-house is anchored to the (Bip!) main chassis itself, and hence the possibility of all sorts of damage.

"Goddamn it, Scott—"

The least dangerous thing that could have gone wrong would have been a random buildup of energies right where Scott had stuck the wire against the housing. Which I guess is what happened because he kept reaching for it and jerking his hand away, like he was being tickled.

Mabel got at the controls and pulled the arm of the rheostat slowly down. She has a blanket ban on all current, and could walk it down to nothing. (All the voltage in the world won't do a thing if there're no amps behind it.) "They know damned well I don't like to waste power!" she snapped. "All right, you silver-plated idiots," she rumbled about the mountain, "get inside. That's enough for today."

She was mad. I didn't pursue the conversation.

Born out of time, I walked eye-deep in Gila droppings. Then I sat for a while. Then I paced some more. I was supposed to be filling out forms in the navigation office, but most of the time I was wondering if I wouldn't be happier shucking silver for denim to go steel wool the clouds. Why grub about the world with dirty demons when I could be brandishing my resentments against the night winds, beating my broomstick (as it were) across the evening; justifying the ways of angels, if not gods, to ... only all my resentments were at Mabel.

A break on the balcony from figure flicking.

And leaning on the rail, this, over-looked and -heard:

Sue and Pitt stood together on the rim of the trough.

"Well, I'll tell you," Sue was saying, "I like working here. Two years in the Academy after high school and you learn all about Power Engineering and stuff. It's nice 'cause you do a lot of traveling," Sue went on, rather like the introduction to the Academy Course of Study brochure. Well, it's a good introduction. "By the way," she finished, and by the way she finished, I knew she'd been wondering awhile, "what happened to your friend's eye?"

Pitt hoofed at the dirt. "Aw, he got in a fight and got it hurt real bad."

"Yeah," Sue said. "That's sort of obvious." The two girls looked off into the woods. "He could really come out here. Nobody's going to bother him."

"He's shy," Pitt said. "And he doesn't hear good."

"It's all right if he wants to stay back there."

"It would be nice to travel around in a healer monster," Pitt said. "I'd like that."

"You want to go inside—?"

"Oh, no! Hey, I gotta get back up on High Haven." And Pitt (maybe she'd seen me on the balcony) turned and ran into the trees.

"Good-bye!" Sue called. "Thank your friend for riding me all around the mountain. That was fun." And above the trees I saw a broomstick break small branches.

I went back into the office. Mabel had come

48

in and was sitting on my desk, looking over the forms in which I'd been filling.

I sorted through various subjects I might bring up to avoid arguing with the boss.

"It takes too much energy to sort out something we won't argue about," Mabel said. "Shall we finish up?"

"Fine. Only I haven't had a chance to argue."

"Go on."

"You go on. The only way I'll ever get you is to let you have enough cable to strangle yourself."

She put the forms down. "Take you up on that last bit of obvious banality for the day: suppose we put the outlets and lines in? They certainly don't have to use them if they don't like."

"Oh, Mabel! The whole thing is a matter of principle!"

"I'm not strangling yet."

"Look. You *are* the boss. I've said we'd do it your way. Okay. I mean it. Good night!" Feeling frustrated, but clean and silver, I stalked out.

Frank Faltaux once told me that the French phrase for it is *l'esprit d'escalier*—the spirit of the backstairs. You think of what you *should* have said after you're on the way down. I lay in the hammock in my new room fairly blistering the varnish on the banister.

Evening shuffled leaves outside my window and slid gold poker chips across the pane. After much restlessness, I got up and went outside to kibitz the game.

On the stream bank I toed stones into the water, watched the water sweep out the hollows, and ambled beside the current, the sound of the falls ahead of me; behind, laughing demons sat on the treads drinking beer.

Then somebody called the demons inside, so there was only the evening and water.

And laughter above me . . .

I looked up the falls.

Fidessa sat there, swinging her sneaker heels against the rock.

"Hello?" I asked.

She nodded and looked like a woman with a secret. She had jumped down and started over the rocks.

"Hey, watch it. Don't slip in the—"

She didn't.

"Blacky!"

"Eh . . . what can I do for you?"

"Nothing!" with her bright brown eyes. "Do you want to come to a party?"

"Huh?"

"Up on High Haven."

Thought: that the cables had not gone up there this afternoon had been mistaken for a victory on my part.

"You know I haven't won any battles down here yet." Oh, equivocatious "yet." I scratched my neck and did other things that project indecision. "It's very nice of you and Roger to ask me."

"Actually, *I'm* asking you. In fact"—conspiratorial look—"why don't you bring one of your

girls along?" For a whole second I thought it
was a non-ulterior invitation. "Roger might be
a little peeved if he thought I just came down
to drag you up to an angel blast."

Tall, very dark, and handsome, I've had a fair
amount of this kind of treatment at the hands
of various ladies even in this enlightened age.

So it doesn't bother me at all. "Sure. Love to
come."

My ulterior was a chance to drag Mabel out
to see my side (as devils stalked the angels'
porches . . . I slew the thought).

Then again, I was still feeling pretty belligerent. Hell, who wants to take your debate rival
to a party.

I looked back at the monster. Sue sat at the
top of the steps, reading.

"Hey!"

She looked up. I made come-here motions.
She put down the book and came.

"What's Scott doing?"

"Sleeping."

One of the reasons Scott will never be a devil
is that he can sleep anywhere, any time. A devil
must be able to worry all night, then be unable
to sleep because he's so excited about the so-
lution that arrived with the dawn. "Want to go
to a party?"

"Sure."

"Fidessa's invited us up to High Haven.
You'll have a chance to see your friend Pitt
again."

She came into the scope of my arm and set-

51

tled her head on my shoulder, frowning. "Pitt's a funny kid." The passing wrinkles on a seventeen-year-old girl's face are charming. "But I like her." She looked up, took hold of my thumb, and asked, "When are we going?"

"Now," Fidessa said.

We climbed.

"Ever fly a broomstick?" Fidessa asked.

"I used to fly my wife back and forth to classes when I was at the academy," I admitted. (Interesting I've managed to put that fact out of this telling so long. Contemplate that awhile.) "Want me to drive?"

With me at the steering shaft, Sue behind me chinning my scapula, and Fidessa behind her, we did a mildly clumsy takeoff, then a lovely spiral—"Over there," Fidessa called—around the mountain's backbone and swung up toward the gorge.

"Oh, I love riding these things!" Sue was saying. "It's like a roller coaster. Only more so!"

That was *not* a comment on my flying. We fell into the rocky mouth. (One doesn't forget how to ride a bicycle, either.) Our landing on the high porch was better than Roger's.

I found out where they did the cooking I'd smelled that morning. Fidessa led us up through the trees above the house. (Roast meat . . .) Coming through the brush, hand in hand with Sue, I saw our late cadet wrinkle her nose, frown: "Barbecued pork?"

They had dug a shallow pit. On the crusted, gleaming grill a pig, splayed over coals, looked

up cross-eyed. His ears were charred. The lips curled back from tooth and gap-tooth. He smelled great.

"Hey," Roger called across the pit. "You come up here this evening? Good!" He saluted with a beer can. "You come for the party?"

"I guess so."

Someone came scrabbling up the rock carrying a cardboard crate. It was the red-headed kid with the dragon on his chest. "Hey, Roger, you need some lemons? I was over in Hainesville, and I swiped this whole goddamn box of lemons—"

Someone grabbed him by the collar of his leather jacket with both hands and yanked it down over his shoulders; he staggered. The crate hit the edge of the pit. Lemons bounced and rolled.

"God damnit, cut that out—"

Half a dozen fell through the grate. Somebody kicked the carton, and another half dozen rolled down the slope.

"Hey—"

Half a minute into a free-for-all, two cans of beer came across. I caught them and looked up to see Roger, by the cooler, laughing. I twisted the tops off (there was a time, I believe, when such a toss would have wreaked havoc with the beer—progress), handed one to Sue, saluted.

Fidessa had maneuvered behind Roger. And was laughing too.

Sue drank, scowled. "Say, where is Pitt?"

"Down at the house."

She flashed bright teeth at me. I nodded.

"Call me when food's on." She pulled away, skirting tussling angels, and hopped down the rocks.

Where does the mountain go when it goes higher than Haven?

Not knowing, I left the revelers and mounted among the bush and boulders. Wind snagged on pines and reached me limping. I looked down the gorge, surveyed the crowded roofs of Haven, sat for a while on a log, and was peaceful.

I heard feet on leaves behind, but didn't look. Fingers on my eyes and Fidessa laughing. I caught one wrist and pulled her around. The laugh stilled on her face. She, amused, and I, curious, watched each other watch each other.

"Why," I asked, "have you become so friendly?"

Her high-cheeked face grew pensive. "Maybe it's because I know a better thing when I see it."

"Better?"

"Comparative of *good*." She sat beside me. "I've never understood how power is meted out in this world. When two people clash, the more powerful wins. I was very young when I met Sam. I stayed with him because I thought he was powerful. Does that sound naive?"

"At first, yes. Not when you think about it."

"He insisted on living in a way totally at odds with society. That takes . . . power."

I nodded.

"I still don't know whether he lost it at the

54

end. Maybe Roger simply had more. But I made my decision before they rumbled. And I ended up on the right side."

"You're not stupid."

"No, I'm not. But there's another clash coming. I think I know who will win."

"I don't."

She looked at her lap. "Also I'm not so young anymore. I'm tired of being on the side of the angels. My world is falling apart, Blacky. I've got Roger; I understand why Sam lost, but I don't understand why Roger won. In the coming battle, you'll win and Roger will lose. That I don't understand at all."

"Is this a request for me in my silver long-johns to take you away from all this?"

She frowned. "Go back down to Haven. Talk to Roger."

"On the eve of the war, the opposing generals meet together. They explain how war would be the worst thing for all concerned. Yet all creation knows they'll go to war."

Her eyes inquired.

"I'm quoting."

"Go down and talk to Roger."

I got up and walked back through the woods. I had been walking five minutes when:

"Blacky?"

I stopped by an oak whose roots clutched a great rock. When trees get too big in terrain like this, there is very little for them to hold, and they eventually fall.

"I thought I saw you wander off up here."

"Roger," I said, "things don't look so good down at the Gila Monster."

He fell into step beside me. "You can't stop the lines from coming up here?" He twisted the great ring on his scarred finger.

"The law says that a certain amount of power must be available for a given number of people. Look. Even if we put the lines up, why do you have to use them? I don't understand why this business is so threatening to you."

"You don't?"

"Like I said, I sympathize . . ."

His hands went into his pockets. It was dark enough here among the trees so that, though light flaked above the leaves, I couldn't see his expression.

His tone of voice surprised me: "You don't understand what's going on up here, do you? Fidessa said you didn't." It was fatigue. "I thought you . . ." and then his mind went somewhere else. "These power lines. Do you know what holds these guys here? I don't. I do know it's weaker than you think."

"Fidessa says they've been drifting away."

"I'm not out to make any man do what he don't want. Neither was Sam. That's the power he had; and I have. You put them lines up, and they'll use them. Maybe not at first. But they will. You beat us long enough, and we go down!"

Beyond the trees I could see the barbecue pit. "Maybe you're just going to have to let it go."

He shook his shadowed face. "I haven't had

56

it long, so it shouldn't be so hard to lose it. But no."

"Roger, you're not losing anything. When the lines go up here, just ignore—"

"I'm talking about power. *My* power."

"How?"

"They know what's going on." He motioned to include the rest of the angels in Haven. "They know it's a contest. And I am going to lose. Would it be better if I came on like Sam? He'd have tried to break your head. Then he'd have tried to bust your tinfoil eggcrate apart with broomsticks. Probably got himself and most of the rest of us in the hoosegow."

"He would have."

"Have you ever lost something important to you, something so important you couldn't start to tell anybody else how important it was? It went. You watched it go. And then it was all gone."

"Yes."

"Yeah? What?"

"Wife of mine."

"She leave you for somebody else?"

"She was burned to death on an exposed power cable, one night—in Tibet. I watched. And then she was . . . gone."

"You and me," Roger said after a moment, "we're a lot alike, you know?" I saw his head drop. "I wonder what it would be like to lose Fidessa . . . too."

"Why do you ask?"

Broad shoulders shrugged. "Sometimes the

57

way a woman acts, you get to feel. . . . Sam knew. But it's stupid, huh? You think that's stupid, Blacky?"

Leaves crashed under feet behind us. We turned.

"Fidessa . . . ?" Roger said.

She stopped in the half-dark. I knew she was surprised to overtake us.

Roger looked at me. He looked at her. "What were you doing up there?"

"Just sitting," she said before I did.

We stood a moment more in the darkness above Haven. Then Roger turned, beat back branches and strode into the clearing. I followed.

The pig had been cut. Most of one ham had been sliced. But Roger yanked up the bone and turned to me. "This is a party, hey, Blacky!" His scarred face broke on laughter. "Here! Have some party!" He thrust the hot bone into my hands. It burned me.

But Roger, arm around somebody's shoulder, lurched through the carousers. Someone pushed a beer at me. The hock, where I'd dropped it on pine needles, blackened beneath the boots of angels.

I did get food after a fashion. And a good deal to drink.

I remember stopping on the upper porch of Haven, leaning on what was left of the rail.

Sue was sitting down by the pool. Stooped but glistening from the heat of the forge, Danny stood beside her.

Then behind me:

"You gonna fly? You gonna fly the moon off the sky? I can see three stars up there! Who's gonna put 'em out?" Roger balanced on the cycle rack, feet wide, fist shaking at the night. "I'm gonna fly! Fly till my stick pokes a hole in the dark! Gods, you hear that? We're coming at you! We're gonna beat you to death with broomsticks and roar the meteors down before we're done. . . ."

They shouted around him. A cycle coughed. Two more.

Roger leaped down as the first broomstick pulled from the rack, and everybody fell back. It swerved across the porch, launched over the edge, rose against the branches, above the branches, spreading dark wings.

"You gonna fly with me?"

I began a shrug.

His hand hit my neck and stopped it. "There are gods up there we gotta look at. You gonna stare 'em down with me?"

Smoke and pills had been going around as well as beer.

"Gods are nothing but low blood sugar," I said. "St. Augustine, Peyote Indians ... you know how it works—

He turned his hand so the back was against my neck. "Fly!" And if he'd taken his hand away fast, that ring would have hooked out an inch of jugular.

Three more broomsticks took off.

"Okay, why not?"

He turned to swing his cycle from the rack.

I mounted behind him. Concrete rasped. We went over the edge, and the bottom fell out of my belly again. Branches clawed at us, branches missed.

Higher than Haven.

Higher than the mountain that is higher than Haven.

Wind pushed my head back, and I stared up at the night. Angels passed overhead.

"Hey!" Roger bellowed, turning half around so I could hear. "You ever done any sky-sweeping?"

"No!" I insisted.

Roger nodded for me to look.

Maybe a hundred yards ahead and up, an angel turned wings over the moon, aimed down, and—his elbows jerked sharply in as he twisted the throttle rings—turned off both turbos.

The broomstick swept down the night.

And down.

And down.

Finally I thought I would lose him in the carpet of green-black over the mountain. And for a while he was lost. Then:

A tiny flame, and tiny wings, momentarily illuminated, pulled from the tortuous dive. As small as he was, I could *see* the wings bend from the strain. He was close enough to the treetops so that for a moment the texture of the leaves was visible in a speeding pool of light. (How many angels *can* dance on the head of a pin?) He was so tiny. . . .

"What the hell is our altitude anyway?" I called to Roger.

Roger leaned back on the shaft, and we were going up again.

"Where are we going?"

"High enough to get a good sweep on."

"With two people on the cycle?" I demanded.

And we went up.

And there were no angels above us any more.

And the only thing higher than us was the moon.

There is a man in the moon.

And he leers.

We reached the top of our arc. Then Roger's elbows struck his sides.

My tummy again. Odd feeling: the vibrations on your seat and on your foot stirrups aren't there. Neither is the roar of the turbos.

It is a very quiet trip down.

Even the sound of the wind on the wings behind you is carried away too fast to count. There is only the mountain in front of you. Which is down.

And down.

And down.

Finally I grabbed Roger's shoulder, leaned forward, and yelled in his ear, "I hope you're having fun!"

Two broomsticks zoomed apart to let us through.

Roger looked back at me. "Hey, what were you and my woman doing up in the woods?" With the turbos off you don't have to yell.

"Picking mushrooms."

"When there's a power struggle, I don't like to lose."

"You like mushrooms?" I asked. "I'll give you a whole goddamn basket just as soon as we set runners on Haven."

"I wouldn't joke if I was sitting as far from the throttle ring as you are."

"Roger—"

"You can tell things from the way a woman acts, Blacky. I've done a lot of looking, at you, at Fidessa, even at that little girl you brought up to Haven this evening. Take her and Pitt. I bet they're about the same age. Pitt don't stand up too well against her. I don't mean looks either. I'm talking about the chance of surviving they'd have if you just stuck them down someplace. I'm thirty-three years old, Blacky. You?"

"Eh . . . thirty-one."

"We don't check out too well either."

"How about giving it a chance?"

"You're hurting my shoulder."

My hand snapped back to the grip. There was a palm print in sweat on the denim.

Roger shook his head. "I'd dig to see you spread all over that mountain."

"If you don't pull out, you'll never get the opportunity."

"Shit," Roger said. His elbows went out from his side.

The broomstick vibrated.

Branches stopped coming at us quite so fast. (I could see separate branches!) The force of the

62

turn almost tore me off. I told you before, you could see the wings bend? You can hear them too. Things squeaked and creaked in the roar.

Then, at last, we were rising gently once more. I looked up. I breathed. The night was loud and cool and wonderful.

Miniature above us now, another angel swept down across the moon. He plummeted toward us as we rode up the wind.

Roger noticed before I did.

"Hey, the kid's in trouble!"

Instead of holding his arms hugged to his sides, the kid worked them in and out as though he were trying to twist something loose.

"His rings are frozen!" Roger exclaimed.

Others had realized the trouble and circled in to follow him down. He came fast and wobbling—passed us!

His face was all teeth and eyes as he fought the stick. The dragon writhed on his naked chest. It was the redhead.

The flock swooped to follow.

The kid was below us. Roger gunned his cycle straight down to catch up, wrenched out again, and the kid passed us once more.

The kid had partial control of one wing. It didn't help because whenever he'd shift the free aileron, he'd just bank off in another direction at the same slope.

Branches again. . . .

Then something unfroze in the rogue cycle. His slope suddenly leveled, and there was fire from the turbos.

For three seconds I thought he was going to make it.

Fire raked the treetops for thirty feet; we swooped over a widening path of flame. And nothing at the end of it.

A minute later we found a clearing. Angels settled like mad leaves. We started running through the trees.

He wasn't dead.

He was screaming.

He'd been flung twenty feet from his broomstick through small branches and twigs, both legs and one arm broken. Most of his clothes had been torn off. A lot of skin too.

Roger forgot me, got very efficient, got Red into a stretcher between two broomsticks, and got to Hainesville, fast. Red was only crying when the doctor finally put him to sleep.

We took off from the leafy suburban streets and rose toward the porches of Haven.

The gorge was a serpent of silver.

The moon glazed the windows of Haven.

Somebody had already come back to bring the news.

"You want a beer?" Roger asked.

"No thanks. Have you seen the little girl who came up here with me? I think it's about time we got back."

But he had already started away. There was *still* a party going on.

I went into the house, up some stairs, didn't find Sue, so went down some others. I was half-

64

way down the flickering steps to the forge when I heard a shriek.

Then Sue flashed through the doorway, ran up the steps, and crashed into me. I caught her just as one-eyed Danny swung round the door jamb. Then Pitt was behind him, scrabbling past him in the narrow well, the throwing blade in her hand halfway through a swing.

And stopping.

"Why doesn't someone tell me what the hell is going on?" I proposed. "You put yours away, and I'll put away mine." Remember that throwing blade I had tucked under my belt? It was in my hand now. Pitt and I lowered our arms together.

"Oh, Blacky, let's get *out* of here!" Sue whispered.

"Okay," I said.

We backed up the steps. Then we ducked from the door and came out on the porch. Sue still leaned on my shoulder. When she got her breath back, she said: "They're nuts!"

"What happened?"

"I don't know, I mean. . . ." She stood up now. "Dan was talking to me and showing me around the forge. And he makes all that beautiful jewelry. He was trying to fool around, but I mean, really—with that eye? And I was trying to cool him anyway, when Pitt came in. . . ." She looked at the porch. "That boy who fell . . . they got him to the doctor?"

I nodded.

"It was the redheaded one, wasn't it? I hope

he's all right." Sue shook her head. "He gave me a lemon."

Fidessa appeared at my shoulder. "You want to go down?"

"Yeah."

"Take that cycle. The owner's passed out inside. Somebody'll bring him down tomorrow to pick it up."

"Thanks."

Glass shattered. Somebody had thrown something through one of Haven's remaining windows.

The party was getting out of hand at the far end of the porch. Still point in the wheeling throng, Roger watched us.

Fidessa looked a moment, then pushed my shoulder. "Go on." We dropped over white water, careening down the gorge.

FIVE

Scott opened an eye and frowned a freckled frown over the edge of his hammock. "Where . . . [obscured by yawn] . . . been?"

"To a party. Don't worry. I brought her back safe and sound."

Scott scrubbed his nose with his fist. "Fun?"

"Sociologically fascinating, I'm sure."

"Yeah?" He pushed up on his elbow. "Whyn't you wake me?" He looked back at Sue, who sat quietly on her hammock.

"We shook you for fifteen minutes, but you kept trying to punch me."

"I did?" He rubbed his nose again. "I did not!"

"Don't worry about it. Go to sleep. G'night, Sue."

In my room I drifted off to the *whirr* of broomsticks remembered.

Then—was it half an hour later?—I came awake to a real turbo. A cycle came near the Monster's roof.

Runners . . .

Correction: landed on.

I donned silver and went outside on the long terrace. I looked to my left up at the roof.

Thuds down the terrace to the right—

Danny recovered from his leap. His good eye blinked rapidly. The other was a fistful of wet shadow.

"What are you doing here?" I asked too quietly for him to have heard. Then I looked up at the curved wall. Fidessa slid down. Danny steadied her.

"Would you mind telling me what brings you here this hour of the morning?"

After five silent seconds I thought she was playing a joke. I spent another paranoid three thinking I was about to be victim to a cunning nefariousness.

But she was terrified.

"Blacky—"

"Hey, what's the matter, girl?"

"I . . ." She shook her head. "Roger . . ." Shook it again.

"Come inside and sit down."

She took Danny's arm. "Go in! Go in, Danny . . . please!" She looked about the sky.

Stolid and uncomprehending, Danny went forward. Inside he sat on the hammock, left fist wrapped in his right hand.

Fidessa stood, turned, walked, stopped.

"What's the matter? What happened on High Haven?"

"We're leaving." She watched for my reaction.

"Tell me what happened."

She put her hands in her pockets, took them out again. "Roger tried to get at Danny."

"What?"

We regarded the silent smith. He blinked and smiled.

"Roger got crazy after you left."

"Drunk?"

"Crazy! He took everybody down to the forge, and they started to break up the place . . . He made them stop after a little while. But then he talked about killing Danny. He said that Sam was right. And then he told me he was going to kill me."

"It sounds like a bad joke."

"It wasn't. . . ." I watched her struggle to find words to tell me what it was.

"So you two got scared and left?"

"I wasn't scared then." Her voice retreated to shortness. She glanced up. "I'm scared now."

Swaying gently, Danny put one foot on top of the other and meshed his toes.

"How come you brought Danny along?"

"He was running away. After the fracas down in the forge, he was taking off into the woods. I told him to come with me."

"Clever of you to come here."

She looked angry, then anger lost focus and became fear again. "We didn't know anywhere else to go." Her hands closed and broke like moths. "I came here first because I . . . wanted to warn you."

"Of what?"

"Roger—I think him and the rest of the angels are going to try and rumble with you here."

"What . . . ?"

She nodded.

"This has suddenly gotten serious. Let's go talk to Boss Lady." I opened the door to the corridor. "You too."

Danny looked up surprised, unfolded his hands and feet.

"Yeah, you!"

Mabel was exercising her devilish talents:

Ashtray filled with the detritus of a pack of cigarettes, papers all over everything; she had one pencil behind her ear and was chewing on another. It was three in the morning.

We filed into the office, me first, Fidessa, then Danny.

"Blacky? Oh, hello—good *Lord*!" (That was Danny's eye.)

"Hi, Mabel. How's the midnight oil?"

"If you strain it through white bread, reduce it over a slow Bunsen, and recondense the fumes in a copper coil, I hear you have something that can get you high." She frowned at Danny, realized she was frowning, smiled. "What happened to that boy's face?"

"Meet Fidessa and Danny, from High Haven. They've just run away and stopped off to tell us that we may be under attack shortly by angels who are none too happy about the lines and outlets we're putting up tomorrow."

Mabel looked over the apex of her fingertips. "This has gotten serious," she echoed. Mabel looked tired. "The Gila Monster is a traveling maintenance station, not a mobile fortress. How have your goodwill efforts been going?"

I was going to throw up my hands—

"If Blacky hadn't been up there," Fidessa said, "talking with Roger like he did, they'd have been down here yesterday afternoon instead."

I projected her an astral kiss.

"What about him?" She nodded at Danny. "What happened to—"

"Where the hell," Scott demanded, swinging through the door like a dappled griffon, "did you take that poor kid, anyway?"

"What kid?"

"Sue! You said you went to a party. That's not what I'd call it!"

"What are you talking about?"

"She's got two bruises on her leg as big as my

hand and one on her shoulder even bigger. She said some one-eyed bastard tried to rape—"

Then he frowned at Danny, who smiled back quizzically.

"She told me," I said, "that he tried to get fresh with her—"

"With a foot and a half of two-by-four? She told *me* she didn't want to tell *you*,"—his mottled finger swung at me—"what really happened, so *you* wouldn't be too hard on them!"

"Look, I haven't been trying to gloss over anything I saw on—"

At which point Mabel stood.

Silence.

You-know-what were passing.

Something clanged on the skylight: cracks shot the pane, though it didn't shatter. We jumped, and Scott hiccoughed. Lying on the glass was a four-pronged blade.

I reached over Mabel's desk and threw a switch by her thumb.

Fidessa: "What . . . ?"

"Floodlights," I said. "They can see us, lights or no. This way we can see them—if they get within fifty meters." We used the lights for night work. "I'm going to take us up where we can look at what's going on," I told Mabel.

She stepped back so I could take the controls.

When the cabin jerked, Danny's smile gave out. Fidessa patted his arm.

The cabin rose.

"I hope you know what you're . . ." Scott began.

Mabel told him to shut up with a very small movement of the chin.

Outside the window, broomsticks scratched like matches behind the trees.

Water whispered white down the falls. The near leaves shook neon scales. And the cable arched the dark like a flayed rib.

Wingforms fell and swept the rocks, shadowed the water. I saw three land.

"That's Roger!"

At the window Fidessa stood at my left, Mabel at my right.

Roger's broomstick played along the still unburied cable, came down in a diminishing pool of shadow directly on the line. I heard runners scrape the housing. Half a dozen or more angels had landed on either side of the trough.

At the far end of the exposed line up near the rocks, dismounted and let his broomstick fall on its side. He started slowly to walk the ribbing.

"What do they want?" Scott asked.

"I'm going to go and see," I said. Mabel turned sharply. "You've got peeper-mikes in here." The better to overhear scheming demons: if they'd been on, Mabel would have been able to foresee Scott's little prank of the afternoon. "Hey! You remember Scott's little prank of the afternoon? You can duplicate it from here, can't you?"

"A high voltage brush discharged from the housing? Sure I can—"

"It'll look so much more impressive at night!

I'm going out there to talk to Roger on the cable. If anything goes wrong, I'll yell. You start the sparks. Nobody will get hurt, but it should scare enough hell out of them to give me a chance to get out of harm's way." I flipped on the peeper-mike and started for the trapdoor. An introductory burst of static cleared to angel mumblings.

Mabel stopped me with a hand on my shoulder. "Blacky, I can make a brush discharge from in here. I can also burn anybody on that line—"

I looked at her. I breathed deeply. Then I pulled away and dropped through to the Gila Monster's roof. I sprinted over the plated hull, reached the "head" between two of the floods, and gazed down. "Roger!"

He stopped and squinted up into the light. "—Blacky?"

"What are you doing here?"

Before he answered, I kicked the latch of the crane housing and climbed down onto the two-foot grapple. I was going to yell back at Mabel, but she was watching. The crane began to hum, and swung forward with me riding, out and down.

When I came close to the cable, I dropped (floodlights splashing my shoulders); I got my balance on the curved ribbing. "Roger?"

"Yeah?"

"What are you doing down here?"

On the dirt piled beside the cable the other angels stood. I walked forward.

"What are you doing? Come on; it's the third time I've asked you." When the wire is sixteen feet in diameter, a tightrope act isn't that hard. Still . . .

Roger took a step, and I stopped. "You're not going to put up those cables, Blacky."

He looked awful. Since I'd seen him last he'd been in a fight. I couldn't tell if he'd won or lost.

"Roger, go back up on High Haven."

His shoulders sagged; he kept swallowing. Throwing blades clinked at his belt.

"You think you've won, Blacky."

"Roger—"

"You haven't. We won't let you. We won't." He looked at the angels around us. "IS THAT RIGHT!" I started at his bellow.

They were silent. He turned back and whispered. "We won't . . ."

My shadow reached his feet. His lay out behind him on the ribbing.

"You came down here to make trouble, Roger. What's it going to get you?"

"A chance to see you squirm."

"You've done that once this evening."

"That was before . . ." He looked down at his belt. My stomach tightened. ". . . Fidessa left. She ran away from me." Hung on his cheek scar, confusion curtained his features.

"I know." I glanced over my shoulder where the office swayed above the monster. In the window were four silhouettes: two women and two men.

"She's up . . . ?" The curtain pulled back to reveal rage. "She came down here—to you?"

"To us. Have you got that distinction through your bony head?"

"Who's up there with her?" He squinted beyond the floodlights. "Danny?"

"That's right."

"Why?"

"She said he was running away anyway."

"I don't have to ask you. I know why."

"They're listening to us. You can ask them if you want."

Roger scowled, threw back his head. "Danny! What you running away from me for?"

No answer.

"You gonna leave Haven and Pitt and everything?"

No answer.

"Fidessa!"

Yes . . . Roger?

Her voice, so firm in person, was almost lost in the electronic welter.

"Danny really wants to run down here with the devils?"

He . . . does, Roger.

"Danny!"

No answer.

"I know you can hear me! You make him hear me, Fidessa! Don't you remember, Danny . . . ?"

No answer.

"Danny, you come out of there if you want and go on back with me."

As Roger's discomfort grew to fill the silence,

the kindest thing I could think was that, just as Danny had been unable to comprehend Sam's brutalities, so he could ignore Roger's generosities.

"Fidessa?"

Roger?

"You coming back up to High Haven with me." Neither question mark nor exclamation point defines that timbre.

No, Roger.

When Roger turned back to me, it looked like the bones in his head had all broken and were just tossed in a bag of his face.

"And you . . . you're putting up them cables tomorrow?"

"That's right."

Roger's hand went out from his side; started forward. Things came apart. He struck at me.

"Mabel, *now*!"

When he hit at me again, he hit through fire.

The line grew white stars. We crashed, crackling. I staggered, lost my balance, found it again.

Beyond the glitter I saw the angels draw back. The discharge was scaring everybody but Roger.

We grappled. Sparks tangled his lank hair, flickered in his eyes, on his teeth; we locked in the fire. He tried to force me off the cable. "I'm gonna . . . break . . . you!"

We broke.

I ducked by, whirled to face him. Even though

the other angels had scattered, Roger had real-ized the fireworks were show.

He pulled at his belt.

"I'll stop you!"

The blade was a glinting cross above his shoulder.

"Roger, even if you do, that's not going to stop—"

"I'll kill you!"

The blade spun down the line.

I ducked and it missed.

"Roger, stop it! Put that blade—" I ducked again, but the next one caught my forearm. Blood ran inside my sleeve. . . . "Roger! You'll get burned!"

"You better *hurry*!" The third blade spun out with the last word.

I leaped to the side of the trough, rolled over on my back—saw him crouch with the force of the next blade, now dug into the dirt where my belly had been.

I had already worked the blade from my own belt. As I flung it (I knew it was going wild, but it would make Roger pause), I shrieked with all rage and frustration playing my voice: "*Burn* him!"

The next blade was above his head.

Off balance on my back, there was no way I could have avoided it. Then:

The sparks fell back into the housing.

From the corner of my eye, I'd seen Mabel, in the office window, move to the rheostat.

Roger stiffened.

He wove back; snapped up screaming. His arm flailed the blade around his head.

Then the scream was exhausted.

The first flame flickered on his denims.

His ankle chain flared cherry and smoked against the skin.

The blade burned in his hand.

Broomsticks growled over the sky as angels beat retreat. I rolled to my stomach, coughing with rage, and tried to crawl up (the smell of roast meat . . .), but I only got halfway to the top before my arm gave. I went flat and started to slide down the dirt toward the line. My mouth was full of earth. I tried to swim up the slope, but kept slipping down. Then my feet struck the ribbing.

I just curled up against the cable, shaking, and the only thing going through my mind: "Mabel doesn't like to waste power."

Gules, azure, sable—

(Working bottom to top.)

"You sure you feel all right?"

I touched the bandage beneath torn silver. "Mabel, your concern is sweet. Don't overdo it."

She looked across the chill falls.

"You want to check out Haven before we go to work?"

Her eyes were red from fatigue. "Yeah."

"Okay. There's still a broomstick—aw, come on."

Just then the chameleon swung up the road-way with Scott, properly uniformed now, driv-

ing. He leaned out. "Hey, I got Danny down to town. Doctor looked at his eye." He shrugged.

"Put it away and go to bed."

"For twenty minutes?"

"More like a half an hour."

"Better than nothing." Scott scratched his head. "I had a good talk with Danny. No, don't worry. He's still alive."

"What did you say?"

"Just rest assured I said it. And he heard it." He swung the door closed, grinned through it, and drove off toward the hub.

A way of life.

Mabel and I went up on the monster's roof. Fidessa and Danny had left it there. Mabel hesitated again before climbing on.

"You can't get the chameleon up the road," I told her.

The turbos hummed, and we rose above the trees.

We circled the mountain twice. As Haven came into view, I said: "Power, Mabel. How do you delegate it so that it works for you? How do you set it up so that it doesn't turn against itself and cause chaos?"

"You just watch where you're flying."

High Haven was empty of angels. The rack was overturned, and there were no broomsticks about. In the forge the fires were out. We walked up the metal stairway through beer cans and broken glass. At the barbecue pit I kicked a lemon from the ashes.

"The devils gain Haven only to find the angels fled."

"Sure as hell looks like it."

On the top porch Mabel said, "Let's go back down to the Gila Monster."

"You figure out where you're going to put in your outlets?"

"Everyone seems to have decided the place is too hot and split." She looked at her bright toe. "So if there's nobody living up here, there's no reason to run power up here—by law. Maybe Roger's won after all."

"Now wait a minute—"

"I've been doing a lot of thinking this morning, Blacky."

"So have I."

"Then give a lady the benefit of your ponderings."

"We've just killed somebody. And with the world statistics being what they are . . ."

Mabel brushed back white hair. "Self-defense and all that. I still wonder whether I like myself as much this morning as I did yesterday."

"You're not putting lines up?"

"I am not."

"Now, wait. Just because—"

"Not because of that. Because of nothing to do with angels. Because of what angels have taught me about me. There's nobody up here any more. I go by the books."

"All right. Let's go back then."

I didn't feel particularly good. But I understood: you have to respect somebody who forces

you to accept his values. And in that situation, the less you agree, the more you have to respect.

We flew back down the mountain.

I landed a little clumsily fifty yards up the stream.

"You liked that?"

Mabel just sighed deeply, and grinned at me a little. "I guess I'm just not made for that sort of thing. Coming back?"

I squinted. "You go on. I'll be down in a few minutes."

She cocked her silver brows high as though she understood something I didn't, but grinned again. Then she started away.

What I really wanted to do was take another ride. I also wanted to get the whole thing out of my mind: well, there were a lot more forms to be filled in. Big choice, but it fixed me squarely at the brink of indecision. I stood there toeing stones into the water.

Sound behind me in the leaves made me turn.

Fidessa, tugging at the pteracycle, one leg over the seat, cringed when she saw me. "It's *mine!*" she insisted with all the hostility of the first time we'd met.

I'd already jerked my hand back, when I realized she meant the broomstick. "Oh," I said. "Yeah, sure. You go on and take it. I've done my high-flying for the week."

But she was looking at me strangely. She opened her mouth, closed it. Suddenly she hissed, "You're a monster! You're a monster,

Blacky; and the terrible thing is you'll never understand why!"

My reflex was to put my hand behind me again. But that was silly, so I didn't. "You think I'm some sort of ghoul? I'm not trying to steal anything that isn't mine. I tried to give it back to Danny, but he wouldn't take—" I reached down to pull it off my finger.

Then I saw Fidessa's eyes drop and realized with guilt and astonishment that she hadn't even seen the ring—till now.

I opened my mouth. Excuses and apologies and expressions of chagrin blundered together on my tongue. Nothing came out.

"Monster!" she whispered once more. And the smile of triumph with the whisper made the backs of my thighs and shoulders erupt in gooseflesh.

Fidessa laughed and threw about her black-red hair. Laughing, she twisted at the rings. The laugh became a growl. The growl became a roar. She jerked back on the rod, and the broomstick leaped, like a raging thing. Bits of the forest swirled up thirty feet. She leaned (I thought) dangerously to the side, spun round, and lifted off. Her high wing sliced branch ends and showered me with twigs and more torn green.

I brushed at my face and stepped back as, beyond the leaves, she rose and rose and rose, like Old Meg, like ageless Mab, like an airborne witch of Endor.

* * *

82

Some history here:

I was transferred at the end of the week to Iguana. Six months later word came over the line that Mabel had retired. So Global Power lost another good devil. Iguana lumbers and clanks mainly about Drake's Passage, sniffing around in Antarctica and Cape Horn. Often I sit late in the office, remembering, while the cold south winds scour the skylight—

Okay, so I forgot to tell you something:

About when I went to look at Roger's body.

He had fallen by the line. We were going to let the Gila Monster bury him when it buried the cable.

I'd thought the ring might have melted. But that hand had hardly blistered.

I took it off him and climbed out of the trough. As I came over the mound, between the brush and the tree trunks, something moved.

"Pitt?"

She darted forward, changed her mind, and ducked back.

"Do you . . . want to take this back to Danny?" I held it out.

She started forward again, saw what I held. A gasp, she turned, fled into the woods.

I put it on.

Just then Sue, all sleepy-eyed and smiling, stepped onto the balcony and yawned. "Hello, Blacky."

"Hi. How do you feel?"

"Fine. Isn't it a perfectly lovely—?" She flexed

her arm. "Sore shoulder." (I frowned.) "Nothing so bad I can't [sigh] work."

"That's good."

"Blacky, what was the commotion last night? I woke up a couple of times, saw lights on. Did Mabel send everybody back to work?"

"It wasn't anything, honey. You just stay away from the trough until we cover it up. We had some trouble there last night.

"Why? *Isn't* it a perfectly lovely—?"

"That's an order."

"Oh. Yes, sir."

She looked surprised but didn't question. I went inside to get Mabel to get things ready to leave.

I kept it.
I didn't take it off.
I wore it.
For years.
I still do.
And often, almost as often as I think about that winter in Tibet, I recall the October mountains near the Canadian border where the sun sings cantos of mutability and angels fear to tread now; where still, today, the wind unwinds, the trees re-leave themselves in spring, and the foaming gorge disgorges.

THE TOR DOUBLES

Two complete short science fiction novels in one volume!